SUGARPLUM DREAMS

Mistletoe Meadows

Book 3

JESSIE GUSSMAN

Contents

Acknowledgments								v

Chapter 1									1
Chapter 2									6
Chapter 3									17
Chapter 4									24
Chapter 5									32
Chapter 6									37
Chapter 7									46
Chapter 8									52
Chapter 9									62
Chapter 10									67
Chapter 11									73
Chapter 12									82
Chapter 13									94
Chapter 14									105
Chapter 15									110
Chapter 16									114
Chapter 17									120
Chapter 18									130
Chapter 19									142
Chapter 20									146
Chapter 21									154
Chapter 22									161
Chapter 23									169
Chapter 24									178
Chapter 25									183
Chapter 26									185
Chapter 27									188
Sneak Peek of Christmas Dreams					197

A Gift from Jessie								203
Escape to more faith-filled romance series by Jessie
Gussman!									205

Acknowledgments

Cover art by Covers and Cupcakes
Editing by Heather Hayden
Narration by Jay Dyess
Author Services by CE Author Assistant

Listen to the unabridged audio for FREE performed by Jay Dyess on the Say with Jay channel on YouTube. Get early access to all of Jay's recordings and listen to Jessie's books before they're available to the general public, plus get daily Bible readings by Jay and bonus scenes by becoming a Say with Jay channel member.

Chapter One

"It's been nice doing the Secret Saint with you," Wilson said as he and Judd Landis finished packing the last Christmas tree onto the trailer where they were taking them to an assisted living facility where children were going to help decorate them on Christmas Eve.

"Same," Judd said as he tightened the strap holding the trees down on the small trailer. Then he straightened. "But I get it. You can't help Charity Ames as well as the Secret Saint as you can as her husband." He paused for a moment then tilted his head. The fading light bathed his face in shadows, and Wilson couldn't see the expression on it. "Did you even ask her if she would marry you?"

Wilson huffed out a laugh. "You know, I've never asked anyone to marry me before. And I can see how guys would get nervous asking someone they've dated for years. But I think that they would have a pretty good idea that she would say yes. For me, I have no idea what Charity is going to say. I've been...dragging my feet about it."

"So that that means...no?" Judd said, and Wilson didn't have any trouble seeing the gleam of his teeth despite descending darkness.

Wilson nodded. "Yeah. That means no." His grin was self-deprecating, although he doubted Judd could see his face any better than he could see his. Which was probably just as well. Judd couldn't see his hands shaking either.

He was trying to do a good deed, that was the thought behind asking Charity to marry him, but that didn't make him any less nervous.

"So if she says no... I'm not losing my partner?"

"No. Although, it might take a little bit before I'm able to talk about it."

"That's okay. We're pretty much done for this year. I suppose I'll have figured out by next year if you and Charity don't get married."

"That would be a pretty big hint." He never even thought about a marriage of convenience until he started this Secret Saint thing, where he and Judd had been helping the more unfortunate members of their little town of Mistletoe Meadows, set high in the Blue Ridge Mountains of central Virginia. But Charity's husband had run off with his girlfriend, leaving her to take care of their five children and a boatload of debt. Charity was drowning, and even though the town had rallied to help her, she was afraid that she was going to be losing her children, if anyone figured out that she wasn't able to take care of them. She confided as much to Wilson, and he wished at the time that there was more he could do.

Marrying her was more than most people would do, but... It seemed like the perfect solution. At least from his end. Maybe Charity wouldn't think so.

He could see a lot of issues, could hear a lot of arguments in his head. Maybe that was why he hadn't talked about it to too many people. He didn't have a choice about talking to Judd about it though, since he wouldn't be doing the Secret Saint anymore, and Judd had a right to know.

"I actually have someone in mind to replace you, if this thing with Charity goes through."

"I had a couple of names swirling around in my head too, but if you've got someone, then you don't need my suggestions." His brother Roland seemed like a good idea. He wasn't married and had a heart of gold, although he seemed a little gruff on the edges. He definitely wouldn't go around blabbing about it.

"I'm open to suggestions," Judd said as he leaned against the side of the truck, looking up at the darkening sky as the stars started popping out.

"It's probably better that I don't have any clue who you decide to choose. It was fun being anonymous. But it did seem like the more people who found out, the more the town knew, the less we were able to do."

"There is a certain freedom that is granted in anonymity," Judd concurred, not the slightest bit offended that Wilson was going to keep his names to himself. As much as he'd love to see his brother get into it, if Judd was going to carry it on, he deserved to choose the person he felt was best for the role.

"I'm glad you're going to continue though. I was kind of upset about the idea of there being no more Secret Saint. And I know the town will be disappointed."

"I might have to quit eventually. I'm married, but we don't have five children. Not yet."

"So how's married life treating you?" Wilson asked, knowing that Judd had just gotten married a couple of weeks ago to Wilson's oldest sister, Terry.

Judd nodded, and a sappy grin that even the weak light couldn't hide split his face. "It's good."

That was all he said, but his tone and his expression spoke far more. Judd was very happy.

"I'd suggest you wait until you find the right person, but I have a feeling that Terry is one of a kind, and no matter how long you wait or how hard you search, you'll never find anyone as good as her."

"I think that's the way a man's supposed to feel about his wife. I know that's the way Terry feels about you."

Judd grinned. But it was true. Even though Terry and Judd didn't really know each other before Terry had moved back to Mistletoe

Meadows to open up her medical practice, and they fell in love quickly, they were just as happy as Amy and Jones who had been friends forever and just realized that they were in love.

Wilson had been just a little bit jealous that Amy and Terry had gotten married on the same day, finding their perfect matches and beginning a life together full of love and joy and happiness.

At the wedding, Wilson had pretty much already decided that he was going to propose to Charity. He wasn't under the impression that it was going to be a love match. Although he had debated about whether or not he should try to court Charity rather than just propose a marriage of convenience which did not sound the slightest bit romantic.

He figured that Charity wasn't interested in a man's attentions, not after what her husband had done to her, and he doubted she was very interested in romance either.

But he didn't know very much about women, not any more than what he learned growing up with sisters and through the few failed relationships that he had in his late teens and early twenties.

"All right then, this is it. It's been fun. And while I don't wish that you get turned down, I won't be sad if we pick up the Secret Saint again next fall."

He grabbed Judd's outstretched hand and gave it a firm shake. "Same. I couldn't have worked with a better man. You have a vision and an ability to seem to be able to do exactly what the Lord wants you to. I've admired it, as well as the upright way you live your life. You're definitely a role model." He didn't usually get all sappy and complimentary, especially with another man, but it was true. Judd had taught him quite a bit in the last couple of years that they worked together. It was interesting to him the way Judd had followed the Lord, and God blessed him not just monetarily, but by bringing Terry into his life too. He didn't think he'd ever seen Judd so happy. In fact, he was sure of it.

Judd slapped him on the back and then walked to the front of the truck, got in the driver's side, and started the engine. Wilson stepped back and watched as Judd pulled out. It was just two days until Christmas, and it was past time that he do what he knew he was supposed to do but had been dreading.

Lord, this is such a crazy idea, I know it has to come from You. I don't know why I'm nervous. If I'm doing what You want me to do, it shouldn't matter whether she says yes or no. But I guess my pride is involved more than I want to admit. It would be a bit of a blow if she said no. But I can't quite bring myself to pray that she'll say yes. I guess, I just need to trust You and know that Your will will be done.

He could always talk to God and say whatever was in his heart. And somehow, just talking to the Lord and letting Him know that and reiterating that he was going to do whatever God wanted him to do calmed him more than anything else could. Not that his hands weren't still shaking, and not that his stomach didn't feel like it was being squeezed by a giant hand, but just that he knew that whatever happened, God was in control. And that was enough for him.

Chapter Two

"Mama, he hit me!" Serafina, Charity's two-year-old, ran up to her, grabbing her leg and crying. She pointed at Evans, her little brother, who toddled along behind her, not really understanding. He was eighteen months old and probably did not mean to hurt his sister. Although, after having five children, Charity knew that it was quite possible that in fact he did mean to hurt her, as little and innocent as he looked.

"Mom! You said I could play with playdough! Where is it!" Lavinia, four years old and not very patient, ever, sat at the kitchen table waiting for her playdough.

It was a long time ago when Charity learned that if she wanted to keep the playdough out of the rug and if she wanted it to last for more than one day, she had to have control over it.

But that meant going and getting it whenever one of her children wanted to play with it, or whenever she had given permission. After all, she wasn't one of those parents who believed that her children should get everything they wanted.

She was, however, one of those parents who believed her

children should have a mother and father and be brought up in a home with both of them.

Unfortunately, Clancy hadn't believed that at all. Or maybe he had believed it, since he explained it to her before they even got married, promising that they would be married forever, which of course, she supposed every man did. After all, the wedding vows said until death do you part. She wasn't the first woman who had been shocked when the man she married had decided that he didn't really mean those vows.

Maybe he had meant them at the time. She could never quite figure that out. Was he deliberately deceiving her all those years? Had he never really thought about whether or not he wanted to spend the rest of his life with one person? Or had he just wanted her at the time and knew that he might find someone else better later?

She couldn't answer those questions. She had never even looked twice at another man after she made those vows and a good while before that. Once she agreed to marry him, she committed her life to him and had zero intention of getting involved with anyone else, ever. She still wasn't the slightest bit interested in getting involved with anyone else, but...her reasoning had changed.

Men were jerks. All of them. She didn't trust a single one. She even struggled to give grace to her own sons at times, although she would never admit that to anyone. It was one of her deepest, darkest secrets. They reminded her of her husband, and while she loved them with her whole heart, sometimes she wasn't sure she liked them.

Was that terrible? She thought so. It made her a terrible mother. Unfit to raise children, except...she loved them too much to let them go.

The state foster care system would be more than happy to take them off her hands. And had in fact scared her more than once by implying that they considered her unfit.

A fit mother should be able to pay bills. A fit mother should be able to keep her husband. A fit mother could find a job that would pay her enough to be able to afford daycare for her children while she worked.

"Mom! I'm waiting!" Lavinia banged her hand on the table.

Gifford and Banks, eight and five respectively, wrestled in the living room, which Charity had almost forgotten, except she heard a bang and then a crash and then crying.

No doubt Gifford, who was much bigger than Banks, had thrown him into something and broken yet another lamp.

Charity wanted to put her hands over her face and cry. That was the last lamp in the house. They did have ceiling lights, thankfully, which the boys had not quite been able to reach, although one ceiling light had been badly damaged by a ball they'd been throwing in the house before Charity had stopped them.

But she couldn't hardly send her children outside to play. She was unable to supervise them outside when she was inside baking for her business. She could hardly be outside watching her kids and inside baking at the same time.

Her mother assured her that thirty, even twenty years ago, it was perfectly okay to send your children outside and tell them to be back in by the time the streetlights came on.

If Charity did that, child services would have them in custody by the end of the next day. Or maybe Charity was just scaring herself, but she wasn't going to take that chance.

Sighing deep and long in her soul, she smiled at Lavinia and said in her calmest voice, "I'll have your playdough in just a moment, sweetheart. Let me go make sure your brother's okay."

"I've been waiting longer!" Lavinia said, all the while pounding her hands on the table.

Charity should really teach her not to pound on the table and to speak to her mother in a more respectful tone, but Banks was crying like he was truly hurt, and she probably ought to make sure that he wasn't dying.

Although, part of the reason she hoped he wasn't was because she couldn't afford the funeral expense.

No, that wasn't true. She loved her children, truly she did. Just sometimes, she didn't like them very much.

She saw blood first. It seemed to be a mother's instinct to zero in on that life-giving substance and another motherly instinct to try to make sure that it stayed within the bounds of her child's body at all times.

But Banks was most definitely cut, and it looked like there was a ton of blood. Surely he hadn't been stabbed by the glass from the lightbulb?

The lamp was in pieces on the floor, and Gifford stood back against the wall, his eyes on her, worried and guilty.

She hurried toward Banks, who struggled to get out of the broken glass.

"Hold still for a second, bud. Let me help you so you don't cut anything else."

"He pushed me and made me break the lamp!"

"Okay. One more broken lamp isn't going to hurt a thing." It wasn't like she was going to be sitting in a chair reading to anybody anytime soon. Nowadays, the only reading she did was to her children at bedtime.

Every once in a while, she had them sit at the table and she would read while they ate. But the days of her being able to sit quietly in a chair and read to her heart's content were long over. She didn't see them coming back anytime soon either.

"Let me give you a hand," she said, helping Banks and brushing the bits of glass off him. They must have taken the shade off the lightbulb while they were playing, since it was clear over on the other side of the room.

"Gifford pushed me!" Banks said as Charity felt a tug on her leg and looked down. Serafina. She had totally forgotten about her as soon as the crash in the room happened.

But she wasn't bleeding.

"I see a gash in your head. I think that's where all the blood is coming from." She spoke almost as much to herself as she did to

Banks. He wasn't going to care. In fact, as soon as he thought that Gifford was getting his just deserts, he probably would stop crying and be excited about going to the emergency room to get stitches.

Hopefully the gash wasn't that bad. It was a head wound, so it was going to bleed a lot.

"My arm hurts!" Banks said, almost as though he didn't even realize that he was crying.

"All right. Let me see it," she said as she sat down on the chair, no light, and pulled Banks close to her. Serafina pushed against her, and she put another arm around Serafina. Not for the first time, she wondered why God hadn't given mothers five or six arms. One for each child. After all, if the Lord was going to give her five children, shouldn't she have an arm for each one of them?

Apparently not, since God had not seen fit to bestow that upon her. She'd been trusting the Lord for her family size, since it made a whole lot of sense to her to do so, and Clancy had seemed to agree. After all, if a person claimed to trust God but then decided that they would make the decisions about how large their family was, was that really trusting God? Were they saying they knew more than He did? Then of course there was also the idea that God said that children were a reward. Wasn't birth control basically spitting in the face of the Lord who might want to issue a reward to His children? Wasn't it wrong to say to God, "No thanks, Your reward isn't my idea of a good thing"?

She shoved all those thoughts aside. It didn't really matter how she got here. And maybe she was questioning everything she ever knew. Maybe she was wrong about it all. Maybe the world was right, and the Bible was wrong, and she had just been deluded. That's the way it looked to her anyway.

"Where does your arm hurt, honey?" she said to Banks as she pulled Serafina onto her lap, who promptly stuffed her thumb in her mouth and laid her head on Charity's chest. Of all of her children, Serafina was the most cuddly, and she would love nothing better than to spend her entire day sitting on Charity's lap, snuggled up, sucking her thumb, listening to stories, or nothing at all.

Charity wished she had more time to spend holding Serafina. She knew these moments wouldn't last long, but her life seemed to be such a dumpster fire that she was constantly running from one thing to another and didn't have time to snuggle the way she'd like to.

"The whole thing hurts. Everywhere," Banks said, and Charity wasn't sure whether he was being deliberately unhelpful, or maybe his arm didn't hurt anymore at all.

"Gifford, go get me a paper towel so we can stop this bleeding." She should have asked Gifford to do that long before now. As a mom, she learned to prioritize things. Blood and broken bones were at the top of the list, and they were the first things to be taken care of.

Maybe that was why she had unintentionally shoved Serafina aside. The child was not bleeding, nor did she have any broken bones. She just wanted to snuggle, which, if Charity were ranking her wants, that would be very near the top. But she learned long ago that a mom didn't typically get to prioritize her wants. Her life was a series of meeting her children's needs and prioritizing those.

Gifford had run to do as she asked, and he was back quickly with a tissue, which wasn't as good as a paper towel, but in hindsight, Charity thought they might be out of paper towels.

A paper towel wouldn't stick to the wound the way a tissue would, but it was better than toilet paper, although, ten years ago, she wouldn't have the slightest idea about that.

It's funny the ways being a mom changed her.

"Thank you," she said as she took the tissue from Gifford and put it over the gash at the back of Bank's head.

"Ouch! That hurts!" Banks said, using his hand to try to swipe the tissue away.

"I need to press against it so that it will stop bleeding," she said, her tone calm and not irritated. And then Banks smacked at her arm, causing it to push against Serafina who tumbled off her lap and promptly started screaming.

"Stop it! First of all, you don't hit your mother, and secondly, you hurt your sister!" She had been calm up until that point, but her voice was raised as she spoke to her child.

She wasn't as gentle as she could be as she shoved the tissue against the back of his head, holding his forehead with one hand to stabilize it and allow her to get enough pressure against it. They had blood all over the chair.

"Maybe this isn't a good time?" A deep voice sounded, and she looked up to see a man standing in the doorway of her living room.

Lavinia was beside him, and Charity realized she had lost track of her. Maybe the man had knocked on the door and Lavinia had answered it, inviting him in.

"No. It's not a good time. Sorry."

"I'm sorry. I can...go, except—"

She was having trouble listening to the man, because she was barely able to hear him over Serafina's crying and Banks's yelling and Evans's whining to be picked up.

"You're hurting me!" Banks shouted, trying to rip away from her, forcing her to stand, pressing his head into her stomach while she continued to put pressure on the back of his head.

If things had been less chaotic, she might have tried to talk him into sitting still so that she could do it, but right now, she was trying to keep him from bleeding to death or at least from dripping blood all over the house, and her superior strength came in handy.

Out of the corner of her eye, she saw movement, and the man, who she thought she recognized as Wilson McBride, strode into the room and picked up Serafina who had tried to crawl after Charity so that she could grab her legs and fuss to be picked up. He scooped up Evans in his other arm and walked out of the room holding her children.

She wanted to stop him. Where was he going anyway? Did he work for child services?

Maybe she should just let her kids go. Maybe she couldn't take care of them. Maybe they were right after all.

She didn't want to admit to failure, but more than that, she loved her kids. She wanted to be able to take care of them. She wanted to be able to give them every good thing, and she didn't think that anyone could raise them any better than her, not to mention their young lives had already been upended when their father had moved out, and not only skipped town but had gone to a completely different country. With his girlfriend. She was the last bit of stability they had in their lives.

Not that she was doing a very good job.

"I have to put pressure on this so that it stops bleeding. We need to be able to see whether or not you need to go to the hospital and get stitches."

"I don't want stitches!" Banks shouted, his words muffled since his face was still pressed against her stomach.

"I didn't mean to knock him down. We were wrestling. It was an accident," Gifford said, even though she hadn't asked, hadn't accused him of anything, and hadn't even looked at him.

"The man wanted in. I just answered the door." Lavinia spoke up, almost as though she knew that she probably shouldn't have invited the man in to see the chaos that was her family. Although, did her children think this was normal?

Unfortunately, stuff like this happened almost on a daily basis. Bumps and bruises for sure, scrapes and falls of course, and yes, gashes that bled. Crying, chaos, unfortunately, that was pretty much her life.

She supposed she shouldn't be embarrassed that Wilson McBride had seen it. But there was still a part of her that wanted to look like she was put together and an even deeper part of her that wanted to keep her children from being swept away by child services.

"It's okay, Gifford. I know accidents happen. And you didn't mean to hurt your brother." She looked down at Lavinia. "Maybe it will be a good idea for you if you hear someone at the door, you come tell me."

"I did. But you didn't get my playdough, and you didn't answer me when I told you there was someone at the door. So I just answered it myself."

That was probably true, although Charity couldn't remember Lavinia saying anything about anyone at the door. Of course, with all the chaos going on in the house, that didn't mean it didn't happen.

She looked down, tilting Banks's head and carefully lifting the tissue from the back of it. As she had known it would, it had stuck to the wound, and she ended up ripping the tissue.

At least no new fresh blood stained it, and she thought that perhaps they would get away with not having to get it stitched up.

"I'm going to need you to sit down at the table and hold this against the back of your head, okay, Banks?" she said.

"I want you!" he whined and shoved his head back into her stomach.

One second, he didn't want to have anything to do with her and was yelling at her, pushing her away, and the next second, he didn't want anyone to touch him except her and didn't want to take care of himself.

Children could give a person whiplash. But she kind of understood. She felt like that at times too. One second, she wanted one thing, and the next second, she didn't want that at all but something completely different.

Unfortunately, it didn't seem to be something that a person grew out of. But divorce made it worse. That was for sure.

"Let me see what Mr. Wilson wants, and then I will come back and help you."

"You always say you'll come back, and you never do," Banks said as she started moving toward the opening through which Mr. Wilson had walked through.

Banks's words cut. She tried not to let it show, but she recognized the truth in them, even as she wanted to deny it. She didn't take care of her children the way she wanted to. She sometimes did forget to honor her promises, and she hated that. She wanted her children to learn that they could trust her when she said something. That they could take her words and count on them. The way they couldn't count on their dad.

She wanted to be different, but it sounded like she ended up being exactly the same.

She felt weary, the whole way to her soul, but she sat her son down at the table, put his hand over the back of his head and told him to hold it, grabbed the playdough from the container in the dining room, set it on the table in front of Lavinia, opened it, ignored her when Lavinia protested that she wanted pink and not green, and then walked into the kitchen where Wilson had made himself at home, sitting at the table, Serafina on one knee, Evans on the other, and she couldn't quite hear what he was saying to them, but he had made them both laugh.

"Thank you for taking them. I can get them now," she said, holding her hands up for evidence.

The little boy, so much like his father, looked up at her like he didn't know her, put his shoulder out, like he was pushing her away with his body, and laid his head on Wilson's shoulder.

She didn't want to think that he was like his father, but that was exactly what Clancy had done to her.

She tried to pretend she wasn't embarrassed by the fact that her own child didn't want her as she shifted toward Serafina, who could be counted on to always want her mom.

Serafina shook her head no, her thumb going in her mouth and her head lying against Wilson's neck.

He'd had them all of five minutes, and both of her children didn't want her anymore.

Maybe that was the sign that she needed to show that she really wasn't fit to be their mother, and she should just give them all up.

"I'm sorry. Apparently they want to stay on your lap. But I can take them if you want me to."

"They're just fine. I came to talk to you, but I see that this wasn't a very good time. It's...not exactly an emergency, but I kind of wanted to get it said. Since...I'm here now."

"All right. What is it?"

"Actually, you can go ahead and finish taking care of everything you need to do. I would like to have some privacy."

"Well, I have five children, and this is all the privacy you are going to get." She didn't mean to be rude, but she knew the words came out kind of snippy. What did this dude think? That she was just going to...send her kids into the living room and they were all going to all of a sudden behave? This was her life. This was the way they acted. Of course, she probably could turn the TV set on, and all but Evans would be glued to it. She tried not to depend on that for a babysitter, but sometimes she was just so overwhelmed that she had no choice.

$\mathcal{W}$ilson held a young child on each knee and sat awkwardly at the table. This was not going the way he had anticipated.

His thought was that he would knock on the door, Charity would answer, and she would step outside while he presented all the finer points of his plan, convincing her that a marriage of convenience was in her best interest. And that would be it. They'd get married within the next few days, and her children would have a father and she would have a protector and provider and he would be doing the good deed of a lifetime.

Was that really what he thought he was going to do? Swoop in and be the savior here?

Seemed like one man wasn't nearly enough for all the chaos and problems that he'd seen just in the ten minutes that he'd been sitting here.

"That's fine. Would you like to talk about it right here?" he asked, trying to sound calm. She just told him that this was all the privacy they were going to get. And he understood what she was saying. She couldn't just leave her kids. Although, he kind of figured she could probably step outside for a few minutes.

But whether it was because she didn't want to, or because she really was concerned about leaving her children, he could go with the flow. Something told him that he was going to have to learn to go with a lot of flows if this plan worked out.

This is how You're going to shape me, Lord? Send me into a family with five small children and a woman who...is a little bit more stubborn than she seemed last time I'd been in her vicinity?

He knew her from church, although they didn't exactly run in the same circles. She was, of course, involved in all things children, while he, a bachelor with no children of his own, was not.

He had plenty of nieces and nephews, but somehow, it never seemed to be as chaotic at his mother's house, even when all of her grandchildren were there, as it was in Charity's house this morning.

She lifted a shoulder and looked around. "It really has to be. I have one kid who's bleeding and broken glass that really should be cleaned up, and I ought not to leave kids unsupervised in here until that's done at least."

"I can clean up the glass, if you just tell me where the broom and dustpan is." He didn't mind. He actually enjoyed growing up in a big family, and while he didn't remember the chaos, he remembered the camaraderie, always having someone to play with, and while he did remember having to share, as an adult he knew that having siblings had taught him many valuable lessons about life, loving people the way they were, not being able to change anyone but himself, and knowing that there were other people who were going to be affected by the decisions that he made.

Big families were not popular in America anymore, but maybe that was part of the overall problem. Because so many good lessons were learned when people grew up with lots of siblings.

He had never considered how hard it was on the parents to raise such big families though.

"It's behind the door right there. If you don't mind?" she asked, and he'd be willing to bet that she didn't typically put her guests to work, but today seemed to be an anomaly. Maybe guests didn't typically show up when she had someone bleeding.

"I'll get it," he said, standing and realizing that he had one child in each hand. How was he going to work a broom and dustpan?

"Serafina," Charity said, holding out her hands. This time, the little girl went. He'd felt bad for Charity last time when she tried to get her to go and she wouldn't. He figured it was probably just the newness of someone else making the little girl want to stay and giggle with the silly story he'd been telling her.

As soon as she went, the little boy in his other arm started fussing for his mother as well.

"I can take him, but if you don't mind?" Charity said, lifting her brows.

"I don't mind at all. Although I was wondering how I was going to work a broom with two kids in my arms, I think I can do it with just one."

She nodded, barely cracking a smile. She'd probably figured out a long time ago how to sweep and hold kids and probably do dishes and stand on her head at the same time too, if the chaos in the house was any indication.

"Just you and me, kiddo," he said to the little boy as he walked toward the door where Charity had indicated the broom was. The kid stared at him with big eyes, and Wilson made a face, causing him to laugh.

He'd always been pretty good with his nieces and nephews, but he supposed it was a little different when a person could get tired of them and leave, versus being forced to stay forever and ever, amen.

Thinking about it like that, it seemed like a pretty big responsibility, and he wondered again if maybe he hadn't thought it all through.

But once more he was reminded that God had clearly shown him that this was the way he should be going. Still, just because he knew what the Lord wanted didn't mean that he was going about it in the right way. Was there a better way?

God was silent on this. Sometimes it seemed that God's silence meant that maybe he just needed to look around and figure some things out. After all, God had given him a brain, and He probably expected him to use it.

It was a little harder than he thought, juggling the kid and the broom and the dustpan and getting all the glass swept up. He dropped it once and had to start again. The boy wiggled in his arms, and he almost set him down, but he wasn't sure whether he could keep him out of the glass or not, so he wrestled the boy with one hand and the broom with the other. It seemed like neither hand was winning.

"Here. Let me give you a hand with that." Charity's voice came from behind him as he dropped the dustpan for the second time.

Turning, he saw she had her hand out for the young boy.

With the daughter in her other hand, she couldn't grab him securely, so Wilson took the boy by the arms and put him next to her so she could just wrap her arm around him.

She was closer than he expected, and... It felt odd.

He didn't have time to dwell on it though, since there was the glass cleanup and the talk after that he had to get through.

"Thank you. I guess I'm not used to wrangling two things at once."

"No problem. I was able to grow into it, and I think it's easier than having it dumped upon you. You don't have to clean that up. I can set these guys down and do it myself."

"I have it," he said. He wanted to be able to talk to her, and with the glass on the floor, she wouldn't be comfortable.

With two hands, he was able to do it in just a few seconds, and he practically followed Charity back out to the kitchen.

"I take it the blood stopped?" he asked, walking to the garbage can that he'd spotted earlier.

"I think so. I was afraid he was going to need stitches, but I think he's going to be okay."

"You said that so calmly." He was teasing a little. Obviously she was used to things not going the way she expected them to.

"I wasn't being very calm when you came in."

"I noticed." He wasn't sure what to say. He could hardly deny that she'd been yelling at her child. After seeing the chaos in the house, he couldn't blame her. In fact, if anything, he would have to ask how she was able to be so sane despite all the craziness around her. "Is that the way it usually is?" He couldn't help but ask. There was a small part of him that said he really didn't want to know. Or maybe it would be better if he didn't know. After all, knowing might make him want to change his mind. And he hadn't even asked her yet.

"Some days it's worse," she said with a forced smile. Like she was going to smile despite everything that had been happening around her.

"I see." He nodded, putting the broom and dustpan back where they belonged and then coming back over to the table where she seated herself.

"Please sit down," she said as he stopped beside her.

He hadn't gotten a ring.

How could he just now be thinking about that? Wait, did he need a ring? He wasn't really thinking that this would be a real marriage. Well, a real marriage as in lifetime commitment, yes, but...they weren't starting it the way normal people did.

But he wasn't going to have time to explain all that to her. He figured he would probably be doing well if he managed to get the proposal out without being interrupted.

"Mommy, I want another color!" The girl who had opened the door for him stood in the opening to the kitchen, a container of playdough in her hands as she waved it in front of Charity's face.

"Did you clean it all up and put it back in the container?" Charity asked, sounding a lot more calm than what he felt.

"I did!"

"All right. I'll get you a new color, and then you're going to have to play quietly with it until I'm done talking to Mr. Wilson, okay?"

The girl nodded, glancing at Wilson before she looked back at her mom.

"Excuse me for just one second, please," Charity said, taking the playdough and giving him an apologetic smile before standing up with a child in both arms still.

"I can hold one of those kids for you if you want me to," he offered, realizing that he probably should have offered before she got up.

"I think I have it," she said, already taking two steps toward the door.

"All right," he said, sitting back down from where he'd gotten up in a half crouch.

Several minutes later, she came back into the kitchen.

"Maybe this time, we'll have enough time for you to get it out," she said, laughing a little.

"At least you're not crazy yet. I've been sitting here thinking I would probably be insane with all of this chaos."

"There are days I feel like it," she said.

"Mom, my head doesn't hurt anymore. Can I go play?" The boy who had been bleeding walked into the kitchen, his hand at the back of his head holding a bloodied tissue to it.

"Just sit down and color for a little bit so we don't start that bleeding again."

"I feel fine. I want to take this off." He ripped the tissue off the back of his head, and while it didn't look like it was gushing, there were copious amounts of blood on it. In Wilson's experience, it took a little while before a cut that was bleeding that bad stopped completely.

"Oh goodness, I think you're bleeding again," Charity said as he stood with his back toward her.

"Can you hold the baby, please?" she asked, looking at Wilson. "I'm so sorry."

"Of course, and don't apologize," he said.

She didn't answer but hurried to grab a tissue and guide her son into the other room.

It was a few moments before she came back out, apologizing for leaving him so long. The little boy on his lap was doing just fine, and Wilson said, "Maybe you could tell me his name. I've asked him a couple of times, but I can't understand what he's saying. If we're going to be spending so much time together, I should know what to call him at least."

"That's Evans," Charity said, smiling and appearing relieved that he wasn't upset.

She'd no sooner settled herself than the little girl with the playdough was back asking for a different color. This time, Charity sent her back into the room without getting her a new one.

"If you want to talk to me, you better spit it out fast."

"Will you marry me?"

Chapter Four

Charity blinked at the man sitting across from her. He'd been very patient for the last hour while she dealt with her children and he waited for an opportunity to say what was on his mind.

She had never in a million years dreamed that those were the words that were going to come out of his mouth. Honestly, if she thought about it at all, she would have figured that she would never hear those words again. After all, she had five small children and her first husband had considered her to be such a terrible wife and mother that he grabbed his girlfriend and fled to a different country on the other side of the globe. It didn't get much worse than that.

"I'm sorry. I must have heard you wrong. Could you repeat that?" she said, knowing that he could not possibly have said what she thought he did, but wondering why her brain had clipped his words into something so...crazy.

"Would you marry me? That's as short as I can make it."

"I guess I did ask for short. But it sounded to me like you were asking me to marry you, and I know that can't be what you're saying." She laughed, although it was forced. What in the world could he possibly have said? Her brain wouldn't make the words into anything but a proposal of marriage.

"Well, that's why it probably wasn't a good idea for me to make it short, but you had a good point with us being interrupted."

"Okay," she said, uncertainly. Was he serious? Didn't he know that she was in this predicament because of getting married to some idiot man? Would he know she was never considering the idea of doing that again? There was no way she was getting married again.

"So, I know that things are kind of hard for you, and I had a big speech all planned out, but I've mostly forgotten it."

"I'm sorry. I don't suppose you expected to have to wait an hour to get to talk to me."

"I didn't mind. But in that time, there were a lot of thoughts going through my head, and I wasn't practicing my speech."

"So I guess my biggest question is why? What would make you ask me something like that?"

"It seems to me that you could use a protector. A provider. Someone to help you. I mean, I feel like the town has rallied around you, but there's only so much they can do." Evans was squirming in his lap, and absentmindedly, Charity said, "You can put him down if you want to."

"I think he might be wet."

"All right. I'll change him, but...maybe we should finish talking first?"

"Sure. I just... I feel like this is what I'm supposed to do. I was trying to think of ways I could help, and it just seemed like God brought this answer into my head."

"Don't you want to get married to someone you love? I mean, I don't know you very well, but you've never been married before, have you?" Maybe he had a whole passel of kids he wanted her to take care of. Although, if she were applying for that job, she didn't do a very good job of showing how well she could handle things today.

"No. I've never been married. I have had a couple of failed relationships over the years, things that didn't last very long, but... I just never found someone that I thought would want to spend the rest of their life with me."

She noticed that he didn't say he never found anyone that he didn't want to spend the rest of his life with. That made her think that maybe there was someone else there that he loved, but who loved someone else, so maybe he was just settling for her, since he could never have the one that he really loved.

The thought didn't give her any comfort at all.

"So... You're going to settle for me?" She didn't know how to answer him. She might have five children and not know what she was going to do...

What was she thinking? She had five children, and she didn't know what to do! And here was Wilson, an outstanding, respected man in the community, offering to give her an out. To marry her, to give her kids a father, to give her a husband and a provider and a protector, and she was going to get her feelings all twisted and be upset that she wasn't his first choice?

She should be on her knees grateful, begging him to marry her this second before he changed his mind!

"No. I'm not settling. There's no one I found that I wanted to spend the rest of my life with, and I just kind of came to the conclusion that I'm not the kind of man who gets all mushy about that kind of thing. So, I looked around and tried to think of something that I could do, and God brought this to my attention."

"Just like that?" she asked, her eyes narrowed. Maybe he was a child molester and he had his eyes on her and her daughters.

"Yeah. Just like that."

"Do you have references? And do you have clearances from the state?"

There. That should tell her if he was a serial child molester, although it was no guarantee he wouldn't start.

"You can talk to my mom. You can talk to my siblings. I watch my nieces and nephews. There have never been any complaints. But no, I've never had any reason to get clearances, although I suppose I could. If that's what you want. I don't want you to be uncomfortable."

This was crazy. This man could not be for real. This was just...too wild.

"What would this be called? A marriage of convenience, would you say?"

"Yeah. It's kind of a convenience thing for the two of us. Where each of us gets something out of it."

"What are you getting out of it?" she asked immediately, jumping on his statement. There had to be something that he was getting, although she couldn't picture a thing.

"Well, I don't want to sound pompous and arrogant, but I'd feel like I'm doing a good deed, and I don't mean that in a derogatory or I'm putting you down kind of way. It's just... This is an opportunity to help, I want to capitalize on that."

She stared at him. Really? He just saw an opportunity to help, so he offered marriage? Who does that?

"Forgive me if that doesn't sound the slightest bit believable," she finally murmured, ignoring the fact that Lavinia was back in the room asking for playdough again. And Banks was back in telling her that the bleeding had stopped. Even though she told him to stay on the seat and not get up. She'd given him crayons and paper, although neither one of her boys were much into coloring.

She took a breath, trying to drown out the chaos and think. She had to make a decision. Or did she?

"How soon do you need an answer?" she asked, all the while her brain was smacking her up alongside the head telling her to just say yes already. It wasn't like she was expecting a better offer anytime soon.

His brows went up like he wasn't expecting that, and then he lifted his shoulder. "I guess it doesn't matter. I suppose I was thinking we would be married by Christmas, but it's totally up to you. I don't want to push you into something you don't want. But if we're going to do it, I don't see any point in waiting." He kind of grimaced. "I know that's not very romantic. That's the thing that bothered me more than anything. It's more like a business proposition than anything else."

"I don't want romance."

He nodded like he was expecting her to say that.

She laughed a little. "I suppose after what my husband did to me, you can understand that. He was romantic, we dated like every other American couple, and yet still, it wasn't enough to keep him here. I'm not interested in that kind of relationship again. I want something that's going to stand. And matters of the heart don't seem to get you very far when you're trying to stick."

She didn't know if she explained that very well, but he seemed to understand.

"I've watched people get married, and they get divorced. I guess my sister is one of those people. And I'm not sure that I agree that all those feelings are necessary or indicative of whether or not you're going to stay together. You can feel a feeling as strong as it can be, and yet your marriage doesn't last. I don't want a marriage like that. And I suppose when I came here asking, I thought you were the kind of person who was going to stick no matter what. That's what I was looking for more than anything."

She blinked at him. She'd never heard anyone say anything like that before. But he was right. She remembered when his sister Isadora had fallen head over heels in love with the man she eventually married. They had been infatuated to the point of saturation. She wasn't sure she'd ever seen two people more "in love." And yet... That marriage didn't last. It must not matter how in love a person was, just like Wilson had said. Why hadn't she figured that out?

Of course, it was too late for her. She'd been married before Isadora. So she couldn't have learned anything from that, except... she could learn now? She could put it to use in this situation.

Wilson was an upright man with a great reputation in town.

She'd never heard anything bad about him, although it wasn't like she knew him intimately.

"I have to say I agree," she said, realizing it was her turn to talk.

He lifted his shoulder and shrugged a little bit. "I don't mean to not be romantic. But I guess I think that the romance should come after the marriage. Is that crazy?"

"Maybe a little. I think that part of the idea of being able to convince a woman to marry you is to show her how you're going to treat her after you marry her." He didn't need to say anything, because she continued, "So many times, I think a man exhausts his ability to be romantic before the marriage and then after the marriage forgets that was the point."

"Yeah, it's almost like I got her, now I can ignore her. Or maybe you get tired of each other, I'm not sure."

"I guess you could speculate about it all day, but I think it just comes down to two people committing to each other and determining to follow through, no matter what happens."

"And then you have to put guards up around yourself so that you're not tempted away from what you have committed to," she said, believing that with her whole heart. It was a matter of making sure that you didn't cross any lines, and a lot of times, the way to keep from crossing lines was to stay far, far away from the lines.

"I suppose you're talking from experience?" he said, picking Evans up who was clamoring at his knee, and bouncing him there.

Charity had put her arm around Lavinia who had come back out to the kitchen, probably just wanting attention, although it was almost time for lunch. She needed to get the place cleaned up, make sure Banks wasn't still bleeding, and feed her children. Evans and Serafina and Lavinia would all go down for naps.

She could take a nap too. Banks had just turned five and wasn't in kindergarten yet, and Gifford didn't have school until the new year. She remembered as a child looking forward to Christmas break, but as a mom and adult, she wouldn't mind if the kids only had Christmas and maybe a half a day off for Christmas Eve. They could even go to school on New Year's. It wouldn't bother her at all. Except... She wanted to enjoy her children. And Wilson was offering her a way to possibly do that. She wouldn't be pressed for money and time. Although, she wasn't so naïve as to believe that all of her problems would be solved.

"You see how chaotic it is here. You do realize that it's like this pretty much every day, right? I mean, I don't always have blood on my hands and broken glass on the floor, but normally there is crying and fighting and fussing and whining and whimpering and all that, all day long." As much as she would like to just accept his offer and jump in before he understood exactly what he was getting himself into, she didn't want to go through another man leaving her. It had been almost more than she could bear. It wasn't even that she was so much in love with Clancy, as much as his rejection had leveled her. It had cut her in places that she hadn't even realized he could hurt. Deep down into her soul. And then, to try to get back up and stand on her own feet with her children around her, asking where Daddy had gone, and with Gifford suggesting that it was her fault...no. She didn't want to do that again.

She needed to make sure he was informed.

"You do realize that I grew up in a family of six siblings, right? I have an idea of what it's like to be in a big family."

"You probably don't have a lot of memories of what things were like when you were a toddler. And how difficult it was for your parents."

"No. I understand it is not going to be easy. I'm not trying to waltz in here and pretend that it's going to be. I think you're too smart for that, and I'm not that dumb."

"I didn't mean to insinuate that you were stupid."

"I didn't think you were. I just understand that it's not all going to be peaches and roses."

"I don't think it's ever peaches and roses."

"Maybe when they're all asleep?"

She laughed. "I'm usually asleep too at that point."

"Yes, but the idea is nice."

She laughed again and nodded. Funny that the man could come in here and have her laughing. Maybe that was what convinced her. Maybe it was the idea that they didn't have to take things seriously, and he wasn't going to get anxious and upset. Demand things. But instead they could find humor in things.

"Do you like to laugh?" she asked, knowing it was a stupid, sappy question, but one that seemed really important. In fact, maybe it was the most important question after whether or not he was a Christian, but she knew he went to church, she knew he professed Christ, so any more than that only God could see in his heart. She would have to take him at his word.

"I think it's important. Sometimes I'm not sure how people get through their days without laughter."

"All right then, my answer is yes."

Chapter Five

Wilson blinked.

Just like that? Her answer was yes?

His lips started curving up, and he didn't even try to stop them. He didn't want to appear like he was celebrating exactly, but maybe it wouldn't hurt for her to know that he was happy that she said yes.

"Are you sure?" he asked, still smiling.

"I think with God and with laughter, we can do it. I'm not sure there's any other way."

"I think it's gonna take a lot of hard work. We probably ought not to gloss over that part."

"That's true. God, laughter, and hard work."

"Faith, family, and fun. That has a better ring to it."

"It does." She nodded and then looked at him, questions in her eyes. "All right. Where do we go from here?"

He took a deep breath. He hadn't really gotten any further than this and the general idea that he wanted to get married before Christmas. Or maybe on Christmas. "Do we need to wait?"

"Not for me. I'm ready, if you think this is what the Lord wants you to do, and I don't think He's going to drop a better offer into my lap, so I say as soon as you can, let's do it."

"All right then. I'll have to see what we need, but I'm pretty sure we just need to go and get a license, and then we can get married anytime."

"How soon are you looking at?"

He didn't want to scare her, but he figured he might as well be honest. "Tomorrow? The day after?"

"That's Christmas Eve, Christmas."

"Is there a problem with that?"

She drew back a bit as though surprised, blinked, and then said, "I guess not. Actually, I think if you want to get married on Christmas, we might not find someone who's willing to perform the ceremony."

"I'll see what I can do about that," he said, knowing that the pastor would marry them whenever. He'd already spoken to the pastor about what he was considering, and the pastor couldn't find any verses in the Bible against it. In fact, as he and the pastor had talked together, the pastor couldn't find any verses in the Bible to back up that a couple should be in love before they got married. He didn't need to change anyone's mind, but he did think that maybe modern society had permeated into the church and now the church believed something that wasn't necessarily biblical.

"All right. Then...was that everything?" she asked with a little laugh as though knowing as soon as she said that that the little bit he had said was a lot.

"That's it for now. Although, I hate leaving you. I... You can definitely use some help." He had no idea how she worked around the chaos. Maybe she waited for the kids to go down for their naps, but like she said, he was thinking as soon as the kids went down, he would want to take a nap.

"It's okay. I'm used to it. And I've got some work to do anyway."

"Are you still working from home?"

"I am. And I've been providing some baked goods to the grocery stores in town. They've been very good about putting them on the shelves, and they seem to be popular."

"This time of year, I'm sure they are."

"Yeah, just finding enough time in the day to do everything is the problem."

"This is actually my slow time of year. I got the crops harvested, and all I have to do is feed the animals. Make sure the fences are fixed and take care of anything that's sick. Of course, I have some equipment in the shed I'm working on as well."

"I think a farmer's jobs are never ending."

"That they are." He'd been blessed. He wasn't dependent solely on the farm for his living. He had started a business in college that had taken off, and he'd been able to sell shares in it by the time he was a senior, hire employees, and it pretty much took care of itself, leaving him with a good income. That was how he was able to buy his farm.

His family considered him the "golden boy," but he'd worked his butt off for that.

Speaking of his family, he had known from the beginning that this was going to go over like a lead balloon, especially with his mom. She was already dealing with so much, he hated to drop more into her lap, but he wasn't going to have much choice. She needed to know.

"I'm going to tell my mother, but I probably won't tell the rest of my family until we make some firm decisions."

"We can't really do that until we get the license and know when the preacher can marry us."

"Can we find someone to watch the kids this afternoon, and we'll go for a license?"

"I'm sure we probably could, but I have pies to make. Fifteen of them have to be done by tomorrow dinnertime."

"I can watch the kids this evening while you make pies, and I can give you a hand with them once they go to bed?"

She stood staring at him, like she couldn't quite believe it. He supposed he might have had that problem if he were her, but what did she think? That he was going to ask her to marry him, say that he could see that she needed help, and then leave her high and dry?

That was why he had to give up the Secret Saint. He knew it. Raising five children was not going to be easy. Even if there were two of them. Right now, with her doing it all herself, it was the exact opposite of easy.

"All right. I... I'm sorry. I'm just not used to people offering to help. Five kids is not a walk in the park."

"I guess we'll have some other things to talk about," he said, as her walk in the park comment reminded him that he wanted to know if she would sell her house and move to the farm. Maybe they should talk about that now, although he would have to be okay with whatever she decided.

Deciding that it could wait, he sat Evans back down on the floor and stood to his feet.

"I'll see if Mom can watch the kids this afternoon, and I'll double-check with the preacher to make sure that he's okay with marrying us on Christmas, then I'll be back...by one o'clock?"

"Yes. I'll be ready to go get the license at one o'clock."

She sounded like he had asked her if she was ready to face her execution at one o'clock, although maybe he was in a way. After all, the first time she got married, it hadn't ended well, and she surely had some trepidation about this marriage. She didn't know him nearly as well as she had to have known her first husband, and after what she'd been through, he supposed she was probably extremely leery.

With a nod in her direction and a smile at Evans, he walked out the door. Maybe his heart was a little bit heavy. Because while he was still sure that he was doing what the Lord wanted him to do, he understood now that it was going to be a lot harder than he had originally anticipated. And there was still a part of him that didn't really want to give up the idea that he might eventually find the person who was perfect for him and get married and live happily ever after.

But he pushed those thoughts aside. God could do anything, and he had to believe that. Maybe, God could even make love bloom between him and the overworked, hassled, harried, and rejected mother in the house behind him.

Chapter Six

"I'm sorry, I thought you said Wilson McBride asked you to marry him."

"That's exactly what I just said," Charity said into her phone as she watched her children play in the yard. She sat on the back porch steps and watched them swing on the swing and ride their bikes. They had a big front yard, but there was no fence between the yard and the street, and she was afraid to leave them all there unless she could watch them like a hawk.

"And what did you say? Yes, right?" Her best friend, Kyra, didn't even try to hide the tone of her voice which said that Charity would have been six kinds of fools to say anything but yes.

She almost wished she would have said no just so she could say that to Kyra now. Except, it would have been stupid.

"Yes. That's exactly what I said, and he seemed like he believed me."

"Of course he believed you. What I don't understand is why?"

"That was my question too, although I guess I feel a little offended that you said it in that tone."

"I'm sorry. But I don't want you to think that this isn't a big deal. I mean, you have five kids. And Wilson McBride... He's..."

"I know. Successful. Upright life. An upstanding citizen in the town, a man of character—"

"Handsome. Gorgeous. Yummy. Like, I would not mind marrying Wilson McBride, like today," Kyra said, although Charity was pretty sure she was just kidding.

"I guess I didn't even notice that he was handsome," she said, although she knew that was mostly a lie. Thinking back, she had to say he definitely was. His hair was short, almost a military cut, but he had that sexy stubble on his face. It did not hide his strong jaw and Roman nose. Plus, when she thought about his big hands holding her children, she didn't really care what the rest of him looked like, because those hands that looked so tough and strong were so tender and gentle, and it had made her heart flip over in her chest.

"He has great hands," she said quietly.

"What?" Kyra said.

"His hands. I... I really liked his hands."

"You are so weird," Kyra said, and then she laughed. "But I guess I notice fingers sometimes. Like fingers that are made to play the piano or fingers that seem like they would be really good on a guitar or banjo or that seem to be made for the violin."

"Yeah. Only he had a farmer's hands. You know? Like, I could tell they were a working man's hands. But..." She couldn't tell her friend how amazing they looked holding her son and her daughter. There was just something about them that more than anything else were probably the reason that she said yes.

"Are you sure he's not some kind of child molester or serial killer or something?" Kyra said.

"You tell me. What does the town say?"

"That he's a catch," Kyra said without hesitation.

"That's kind of what I thought. And I think I would be a fool to not take him up on it, even though we didn't talk about being in love or anything like that." And she thought he was kind of right. It didn't really matter how deeply in love a couple was. They could be head over heels for each other and be divorced within the year. After all, if she had to go on the strength of her feelings toward Clancy back when they had been engaged, she would have said they would have lasted forever. In fact, she probably did. But it didn't even last ten years.

"Well, I don't know exactly what's going on, but if he's legit and for real, you hit the jackpot. It might even have been worth the crappy treatment from Clancy, to have Wilson. I mean, he'll be your kids' dad, right?"

"Yeah. I guess we didn't talk about specifics, but I assume that was what his point was." He was going to watch the kids later and said she could make pies. He had said something about how he didn't want to leave everything to her, and he wasn't asking her to marry him just so that he could leave her for the long haul.

"I don't know. On the one hand, it seems like there's something fishy, but on the other, I want to believe that God is finally smiling on you." Kyra's voice had modulated and was soft and caring.

Charity couldn't believe that Kyra had stuck with her. It seemed like being friends with her meant a daily dose of negativity, because there was always something going wrong, and it seemed like there was never anything going right, but she tried not to complain. Tried to find humor in the situation, and tried to laugh at herself. Although, she had to admit that there were days where it was extremely difficult.

Still, Kyra had been a good friend.

"Do you think I made the right decision?"

"When did you say you were getting a license?"

"This afternoon."

"Wow. That's fast."

"I guess I didn't see the point in waiting. Once we've made up our minds to do it, we might as well get it done."

"Is that what he said or is that what you thought?"

Charity tried to remember. She couldn't think whether it was his idea or hers, but regardless, if he had said it, she agreed. "I'm not sure. But it sounds right to me. After all, you know I don't drag my feet. If there's something to get done, we might as well do it. Just sitting around thinking about it makes it that much worse."

She laughed. "I don't know how many times you told me that you live through it twice if you sit and worry about it before you actually do it. And then that just makes it more terrible. I didn't used to understand what you meant, but I finally started thinking about my practice sessions like that. I can put it off and put it off and put it off, dreading it all day long and finally doing the practice session in the evening, or I can get up in the morning, practice, get it over with, and feel good about it."

"Yeah. It's kind of like that. Only, I don't know if I'll feel good about getting married once we do it, but there's just no point in thinking about it and thinking about it and thinking about it and dreading it and second-guessing myself. We made a decision. Let's do it and move on."

"But sometimes when you let some time elapse between your decision and moving on it, things come up that might not have come up if you hadn't waited."

"And that's why I'm asking. Is he a serial killer? Is there something about him that I don't know? Is he really what he says he is? He seems like he's too good to be true. Sometimes when things seem that way, they really are."

"Yeah. And I agree with you completely, except it's Wilson McBride, and I'm pretty sure he's not too good to be true. But if there is a reason that you should say no, surely his mom would know, wouldn't she?"

"I would think that she would. And I'll be seeing her later today."

"All right. Ask her."

"He's going to be there though. I can't ask her in front of him."

"Why not?"

"Um, because he's going to be there?"

"So do you think his mom will tell you the truth while he's there, or do you think that...would hurt his feelings?"

"Both?"

"I can tell you for sure that his mom will tell the truth. She is known even more in town for being upright and honest. If there's a problem, she's not going to beat around the bush about it. But she might not tell you if you don't ask."

"All right. But what about hurting his feelings?"

"Don't you think he wants to be married to a smart woman? Don't you think you'll look smart if you ask his mother whether or not he's a good man? Do you really think that's going to offend him if he doesn't have anything to hide?"

"I suppose that he shouldn't blame me for trying to make sure that I'm doing the right thing." She still wasn't entirely sure that it was a good idea, but she understood what Kyra was saying, that it might offend him a bit, but he should want her to turn over every stone that she could in order to make sure that she wasn't making a mistake.

Although, she supposed that depended on him caring about her, and they weren't really getting married because he cared.

Except, they kind of were. He had seen a need, and he had figured out a way to meet that need, although he also said that he was following what the Lord wanted him to do.

She knew for a fact that the Lord didn't want her to marry a serial killer or child molester, so there was that.

"Are you thinking about it, or are you trying to figure out how to get out of it?" Kyra finally asked when she hadn't said anything.

"I'm thinking." Her eyes landed on her kids. Gifford pushed Serafina on the swing, while Banks and Lavinia rode their bikes. Evans sat in the sand, digging with a shovel. Gifford was old enough to know to watch for Evans to make sure the swing didn't hit him.

She appreciated Gifford most of the time. He had really stepped up and helped with his younger siblings, but she wondered if maybe she was depending on him too much. She also had the nagging feeling that he was like his father. She really had to get over that. She couldn't tell anyone. It was just something that was between the Lord and her, and she needed to get over it.

"I can't think of any reason to tell you not to," Kyra said. "I can think of a whole bunch of reasons to tell you that you should. I suppose the only thing that I would say is just be sure it's what God wants you to do, because you know better than anyone that once you've done it, you can't undo it."

That wasn't entirely true. It could be undone, just not without a lot of pain and suffering, and someone, or someones, had to pay. In this case, Clancy had been able to get out of it, he'd been able to skip the country, but she and the kids were paying. They would probably spend the rest of their lives paying. Especially the children. She would probably get over it, most likely anyway, but things that a child suffered in their childhood would mark them for the rest of their lives. It made her angry every time she thought about it, and if Clancy was standing in front of her, she couldn't guarantee she wouldn't grab him by the hair and body-slam him into the ground. She hoped she was a better person than that, but she honestly wasn't sure.

"Thanks. I guess that's what I was asking. If there was some kind of big red flag that I was missing, that someone else could see and could tell me about."

"If you need music for your wedding, you know my number," Kyra said.

"You're almost done with all of your holiday parties. Are you ready to get your life back?" Charity asked, trying to turn the subject from herself to her friend. It seemed like every time they talked, she took up the bulk of the interactions. She hated that she seemed to do that.

"I'll be happy when they're over, although my checkbook really likes the holiday parties."

Charity laughed. "And I love listening to you. I wish I had been able to listen more."

"We're playing on Christmas Eve. You are planning on coming, aren't you?"

"Yes. Of course. I wouldn't miss Christmas Eve for—" She stopped. If she was married to Wilson, it wouldn't be just her decision. But Wilson wouldn't keep her out of church. Of that she was certain. And that was part of the reason why her decision wasn't that difficult.

He was a believer, quite a strong one from her experience and from everything she heard. That was probably more important than anything, and that was where she had gone wrong with Clancy. He went to church, but only because she wanted him to. And that was before they got married. Once he got married, he didn't feel the need to please her anymore and had stopped going. She supposed that happened to a lot of people, but she resented it. Why had he pretended, when he knew he wasn't going to follow through? They both would have been happier with other people. She'd only wanted someone who was committed to the Lord, or she'd rather have been alone. Clancy would be happier with someone like his current girlfriend, who didn't think anything about committing adultery with a married man and father of five.

If that was the kind of character he was looking for, it made Charity wonder what he had ever seen in her.

"Did you just remember something else you have to do on Christmas Eve?" Kyra prompted when she didn't say anything more for a while.

"No. I just went off on a rabbit trail in my head, but I know that wherever I am with Wilson, he's not going to keep the children and me out of church. And he'll be there too."

"I'm sure he will. He and his family are staples in the church. It would be weird to be there without them."

"They are there every time the doors are open as far as I know," Charity said.

And that was true. They really were there, and that's what she wanted. More than romance, more than everlasting love, she wanted a man who followed the Lord. Even more than she wanted that sexy stubble on his chin.

Although, she wouldn't turn that down.

"All right. I better get going. I have to head in to work. Are you going to be okay?"

"Actually, if this works out the way I'm hoping it will, I'll be more okay in the coming year than I've been in the last ten."

"Yeah. I hope so, and I hope Clancy comes back and you can rub it in his face."

"I don't think so. He didn't have a problem giving up custody of the children and sending the divorce papers. I signed them, they're filed, and that's that."

"Oh, you might be surprised. I don't think he's going to be happy with that bimbo that he ran off with, and when he comes crawling back, you can spit in his face."

"I don't think that I would spit in his face, although maybe that's just me liking to think I'm a better person than what I actually am."

Kyra laughed for a bit, and then after a few more comments, they hung up.

Charity sat on the step watching her children, feeling a little better now that she'd talked to someone. Sometimes she was pretty good at making decisions in her head, by herself, and basing what she thought on the Bible, but the Bible didn't have a whole lot to say about this.

She could point to Isaac and Rebekah as a marriage of convenience, so she didn't think that it was forbidden. Although the Bible didn't label it as such, and their situation was much different than hers.

It did say that to be divorced and remarried was to commit adultery, although Jesus said except in case of fornication, which to her understanding meant that if one of the people in the relationship committed adultery, the other one was free to go. That would be her. And her ex-husband had committed adultery.

She consoled herself with that for a while, telling herself that she was doing what God wanted her to do, even though it was hard. On the other hand, Clancy had stepped completely outside of God's will, and while he might prosper for a season, there could be no good in the end. While she expected to step into heaven and hear "well done."

That did not negate the fact that every day was a struggle. Although times like this, when her children were playing and getting along and not going to her crying every two seconds, were the best times, the happy times, but she supposed she wouldn't appreciate happy times nearly so much if she didn't have those other times.

Glancing at her phone, she realized that she needed to get the kids in and get them settled in for their naps since Wilson and his mother were going to be there shortly.

And she was going to go get a marriage license. For the second time. Hopefully, it would be the last time.

Chapter Seven

"Hey, Mom," Wilson said as he stepped into his mother's kitchen. It was one of those rare times where the kitchen was actually quiet.

"Hey there. I wasn't expecting to see you today," his mother said, looking up from where she was pulling a mincemeat pie out of the oven. The whole house smelled like mincemeat, and Wilson tried not to cringe. Mincemeat was not his favorite.

"I know. I've been...working on a couple of things, and I have a favor to ask of you."

She set the pie on the counter, closed the oven door, and took the mitts off, setting them back in the drawer. She came over to the other side of the bar and faced him across it.

"You know I'm always ready to help you with anything you need me to. What is it?"

"I want you to watch the children so my fiancée and I can go down to the courthouse and get a marriage license."

His mother stared at him. Maybe he should have worded that slightly differently. He didn't seem to be any good at breaking this gently to people. But it wasn't really happening in a gentle way, it was happening lickety-split, and maybe that's the way he needed to break it to people.

"So do you want to back up and start the story from the beginning?" his mother said, calmly, and then she grabbed her coffee from the counter, pulled out a stool, and sat down.

He laughed a little, pulled out a stool on his side of the bar, and sat down facing her.

"Do you need coffee?" his mother asked, knowing that he didn't drink it.

"No thank you. It hasn't gotten that bad yet."

She laughed. But the concerned expression on her face did not waver. "I'm waiting," she said with a tight smile.

He figured she was probably bracing herself. She had so much bad news this year, and he didn't want to be the bearer of more bad tidings, but he didn't figure that she would be overly happy with what he had done. Although, he knew that he could tell her that he felt like it was what God wanted him to do, and while she might not accept that, might ask if he had questioned it, he was pretty sure that if he could convince her that he was one-hundred-percent sure it was what the Lord wanted him to do, she would be okay with it. Not that a person's weird actions could be excused anytime they said it was God's plan. But it did have a tendency to make things go better with his mom anyway.

And it was the truth.

"Well, I've been doing some work this year, and I started to notice a woman in our town, you know her, Charity Ames, and her five children."

"Charity is a really sweet woman. I've noticed her as well and have done a few things for her also. She definitely can use any help that she can get," his mother said, and then she pressed her lips together almost as though she were deliberately not saying anything more.

He almost smiled but managed to keep his face serious.

"I wanted to try and figure out if there was more that I could do for her. She has five children, her husband has left her, he's not wanting custody, not wanting anything, and..." He didn't want to say that he knew that she was behind on her bills and that her mortgage was six months overdue. That she was trying to scrape it together as best she could but hadn't been able to. There were some things that he knew because of his work as the Secret Saint that normal people didn't know. And he didn't want to spread that information around.

"I just know that she's in financial difficulty, she's struggling, and as I was thinking back, I felt like the Lord was nudging me to marry her."

"Really?" his mom said. It was just one word, but it was said in that tone that had all kinds of doubt and questions in it. She was questioning whether or not he was truly hearing from the Lord. And he couldn't really blame her.

"That seems like a really weird thing for the Lord to do, doesn't it?"

"It sure does," she said with not a little bit of sarcasm.

"I suppose Hosea felt the same way."

His mom pressed her lips together once more and nodded at the same time. That was her signal that he just outmaneuvered her.

"I suppose you're right," she said, although this time, there was more humor in her tone than sarcasm.

"I'm pretty sure I am." He didn't mean to rub it in, but that's what he had thought about when he thought that God was being ridiculous—God seemed to work and move in the area that humans considered ridiculous.

"All right. So... What else?"

"So, I prayed about it, thought about it, and talked to the pastor about it, and decided that I might as well talk to her. Maybe she would turn me down. It's kind of out there."

"To say the least."

"Exactly. And I guess there's a part of me that thinks maybe if I keep waiting, I'll find someone. The same way Terry and Amy have."

"I'd really like for that to happen. I kind of thought that Bergen was the one."

"Trust me. I did too. She seemed perfect in every way, except in the way that she didn't want to spend the rest of her life with me."

"Yeah." His mom held a ton of apology and sorrow in that word. She was upset with him for not being able to keep her. She was more upset with Bergen for leading him on for so long and not telling him that she had no intentions of getting married until she had traveled the world. She was just staying in one spot, making enough money to fund her travels.

"So I went today and talked to Charity."

"With the kids there?"

"I think I saw five. Is that all she has?" He was pretty sure about that. He'd been involved in the Secret Saint work that had gotten her children Christmas gifts. He hadn't done it all himself though, so maybe he was missing one.

"That's the number she has. That makes sense, since school is out today. All of them would have been there."

"Yeah. Well, it was chaos."

"That'll be the way it is every day. It's the way five kids are."

His mom would know. She had raised six.

"Well, not to say I was expecting it to be easy, and after today, I know it's not going to be, but more than ever, I'm sure that's what God wants me to do. I just know it in my heart."

"Our hearts are 'deceitful above all things, and desperately wicked.'"

"I'm sure of it in my soul," he corrected himself, since his mom had not argued with him but quoted a Bible verse. No one could do that better than his mom.

"If you're sure, I'm behind you. I certainly don't think God would tell me what He's expecting out of you. You're a grown man, and He's going to talk to you directly, and I trust you to know what He's saying."

"Thanks, Mom." Wilson couldn't tell her how much that meant to him. And he doubted that his mom had said all that was in her heart. She had high hopes for him. After all, he was the one who had created a multimillion-dollar company while he was still in college and then came home and bought a farm and made it successful as well. They were probably expecting more out of him than to marry a woman and take on the raising of another man's five children. Especially when he hadn't dated that woman and wasn't claiming to love her. It flew in the face of everything that pretty much everyone in the United States, including Christians, believed. But he felt like it was the right thing, and he didn't see anything in the Bible prohibiting it. In fact, he could point to more Bible for it than for falling in love.

"You've got a good head on your shoulders, and I know you love God. Whatever He tells you to do, you do, and I'll help you as much as I can."

"Well, we need to go down to the courthouse today and get a license, and I was hoping you would watch her children. Probably at her house. I didn't talk to her about bringing them here."

"It's always nicer to watch them in your own house, but it's probably about naptime for little ones, and they don't know me, so her house is most likely the best place."

"I'll talk to her about bringing them here if we need you again."

"I appreciate that. But if it's not okay with her, I'll watch them anywhere. I guess I'm going to have five new grandchildren for Christmas. God is pretty awesome when He gives gifts, isn't He?"

His heart swelled. Did anyone in the world have a better mom than he did? "I love you, Mom."

"And I love you too, Wilson. And I'm excited about this new chapter in your life. If God is orchestrating it, you know it's going to be good."

"I know it's going to be good, I just hope I'm up to the challenge."

"I know you are. God doesn't call you without giving you everything you need in order to answer that call." She laughed a little. "Sometimes you don't get what you need until the very second you need it, though."

He laughed, but he supposed that he was going to remember those words in the days ahead.

Chapter Eight

"Are you sure she's going to be okay?" Charity asked as they walked away from her house and the door closed behind them.

"She raised six children, so she's used to it."

"She's not as young as she used to be."

"It's just for an hour or two. I don't know how long it will take, and we can hurry right back, although... I thought I would buy you lunch if you wanted."

Her heart flipped. Not just that he was going to buy her lunch, that was really sweet, but he was awkward and unsure, like it mattered to him whether or not she said yes. Like he wasn't sure that she would say yes. Normally she liked a strong man who was confident and sure of himself, but the idea that he showed a little bit of insecurity where she was concerned, that he cared about her answer, that he wanted to make sure that she was happy, it...did something for her. How long had it been since Clancy had cared?

"I would love that. And I left my number with your mom, so she can text or call if there are any problems. Do you think she will?" Some people would just muddle through no matter what, not wanting to bother anyone, and on the one hand, Charity wouldn't mind if his mom did that. She just didn't want his mom to be... overwhelmed. To hate her before they even had a chance to spend time together. Just because her children were so bad.

"I know that if something happens, she won't hesitate to reach out. But I also know that there probably isn't a situation that could happen to her that hasn't already happened."

"Did you guys ever set the house on fire?"

Wilson stopped beside his truck, his hand on the door latch. "No?" He tilted his head. "Is there something you need to tell me about your children?"

"No. I just, you know, thought of a situation that your mom might never have been in before."

"She's never been on a ship that has been sunk at sea, either, but I don't think she's going to have to face either one of those scenarios today. Please tell me that you don't think either one of those scenarios are probable either," he said, and while there was humor in his voice, he was also looking at her, waiting for her answer.

"In my experience, my kids will do anything to make me look like a liar. Not even close," she said, putting her hand up as he opened the door and she stepped in and sat down. "But that's just the way kids are."

"All right. I'll give you that. So you don't want to say for sure your kids aren't going to set the house on fire, because then it's definitely going to happen."

"Yes. That's what I was trying to say."

"All right then. That's good enough for me."

He shut the door and walked around the truck. He wore a button-down shirt but no coat. It was mild, high fifties maybe, and he had the sleeves rolled up and his forearms stuck out. He looked good in his jeans and boots, and she felt like she needed to pinch herself to remind herself that it was real. He really wanted her. Although, the idea that he was just doing what God wanted him to do, while she loved that, it also made her feel...like she was just a part that he was playing and not something he really loved. It was like playing music because he had to instead of because he wanted to.

She tried to push those thoughts away though, because they weren't helpful. So what if he was marrying her because God wanted him to? She loved a man who would do what God wanted over everything. She admired that and was grateful that he was like that.

"The pastor wanted us to stop by for a little bit of marriage counseling, although he agreed to marry us on Christmas if that's still okay with you."

"Marriage counseling?"

"Yeah. He was fine with us marrying, but he said that he usually has people attend several sessions of counseling before he agrees to marry them. In our case, he agreed to waive that, but he still wanted us to stop in."

"All right. So should we do that before we eat?"

"I guess I thought that that was probably best. Not that I want to get the worst thing out of the way, but I guess I just want to get the thing that we have to do out of the way, in case something does happen with the children and we need to go home early."

"That's wise. All right."

He pulled out on the road, heading toward the courthouse.

"So you have a lot of good memories of Christmas as a child?" he asked as he signaled and then checked his mirrors before pulling out and turning.

"I suppose. My parents got into the whole Santa Claus thing, and I was so bummed when I found out that he wasn't real. I truly believed. My sister thought it was hilarious. And I often wished I had a younger sister, because I always thought I would be nicer to her than my older sister was to me."

"Wow. Those are kind of mature thoughts for a kid."

"Yeah, maybe. I just never thought she was very nice. But I suppose looking back, she just acted the way older sisters usually act. I wish I could have been brought up in a big family like yours."

"There were definite benefits to it. But you probably had your own room."

"That's true, I did. But I never really learned to share it. It was such a shock when my husband and I moved in together. I wasn't used to having to share anything."

"There are some good lessons you can learn growing up in a big family. Is that why you decided to have a lot of children? Because you only have one sibling?"

She hesitated. There weren't a whole lot of people who agreed with her or not necessarily agreed with her, just had never thought about things the way she did. She took a breath and then said, "I don't think birth control is biblical."

His brows went way up, and he glanced over at her quickly before his eyes went back to the road. There wasn't a ton of traffic in Mistletoe Meadows at this time of day, but there was enough to keep his attention focused on driving.

"Do you have verses to back that up?"

"I don't have a verse that says thou shall not use birth control, but God talks about how children are His reward. If we're using birth control, we're kind of keeping Him from rewarding us, aren't we?"

"I never really thought about it like that, but I suppose."

"And birth control is just as much for unmarried people who want to commit fornication with no consequences as it is for married people who don't want to be bothered with a ton of kids."

"That's true. There's a lot more of that going on, and I suppose birth control has a lot to do with it. If people were afraid that they were going to have children, they would probably engage in a lot less fornication."

"Yeah. They'd get married younger, have bigger families. And I guess I don't see the harm in that. I know that that kind of flies in the face of everything that society tells us we should do, but the Bible says 'the fruit of the womb is his reward.' God wants to reward us with children. He told Adam and Eve to go and multiply and subdue the earth. He never rescinded that comment, even though some people would think that or tell you that the earth is overpopulated. But I think that God would know that better than men."

"I agree. And you're right about the verses. I suppose I just never thought about it. It's just something everybody does. And having a lot of children is a lot of work. Most people don't want that kind of work."

"I agree. It's all hard work. For sure. And you can end up like me. Believing that birth control is wrong, so then you have five kids, then your husband can't take it anymore, and he flees the country. That... doesn't look very good for my argument."

She was joking a little, making light of herself, and he laughed. It made her happy that he understood that she wasn't ripping on Clancy exactly, and she wasn't complaining or upset. But she could hardly preach it if she wasn't living it, but when people looked at her life, she wasn't a convincing argument.

"So you think birth control is a sin?"

"I looked into it when I was first married because you know that's kind of pushed on you at every appointment you go to. And I found out that a lot of birth control is an abortifacient, or an egg is fertilized, but the lining of the uterus is compromised in such a way that the fertilized egg cannot implant. There are other forms of birth control, but I would say for sure that any birth control that allows an egg to be fertilized but not implant is wrong."

"Wow. You really did your due diligence."

"I didn't want to get to heaven and see a bunch of children greeting me at the gate. Children that I didn't even know I had, because I killed them without even realizing that they had been created."

"That's a sobering thought."

"Yeah. How was I going to explain that to the Lord? I mean, I know He gives us grace, and it wasn't like I thought that God was going to send me to hell if I used birth control. Obviously, that's not biblical, but I do want to try to please the Lord in everything I do. Sometimes that means being more mindful about what I'm doing and not just accepting 'conventional wisdom.'" She used air quotes around "conventional wisdom." And then her hands dropped to her lap.

Maybe she should just keep her mouth shut. If she kept talking, Wilson might not want to marry her anymore.

"Then how do you feel about birth control now?" The question seemed cautious, and she glanced at him.

"I guess I still feel the same. Any birth control that is an abortifacient is wrong. And I guess if God is trying to bless me and I'm trying to keep Him from blessing me, then I'm the one with the problem."

"Can I think on that some?" he asked and glanced over at her. His eyes were serious and thoughtful.

"Of course. We don't have to agree on everything."

"Well, this is kind of an important thing. I… I assume we're getting married, and we're staying married for the rest of our lives, and this is an issue that we're going to have to deal with."

Her heart skipped a beat and then started up again faster, thundering in her chest. She hadn't really meant to bring up that subject, but she supposed it was a good thing he had. She hadn't wondered about it, just assuming that marriage was a marriage, but now she knew for sure.

It made her a little nervous.

She wasn't the young girl that she was the first time she got married.

She felt so much older now. Even though it was only ten years, it felt like a lifetime. That young, innocent girl, who had stars in her eyes and thought she knew everything, no longer resembled her in any way.

"Well, we kind of got off subject. I asked about Christmas, and we ended up talking about birth control."

She laughed. "I'm sorry. I was just thinking that I'm not like the little girl I used to be. Even the young, innocent girl I was when I got married the first time. I'm older, more serious, I have a tendency to think about things, and I guess pleasing God is more important to me than almost anything, hopefully anything."

"I like that. I knew that about you, or suspected it, because of things people had said. It's one of the things I talked to the pastor about. I wouldn't have felt comfortable marrying you if not, although I don't know that God would have told me that I should, does that make sense?"

"God has a tendency to know what we need before we do. And He definitely knew I needed you. And He brought me the perfect man, one who is concerned about doing right and who loves Him above all else."

That was what she wanted, even if she did feel a little bit put out that Wilson loved God more than he loved her, or that Wilson was just marrying her because God told him to.

"You know, I never thought about how Hosea's wife felt."

"Really?"

"No. I mean, it must have been really nice to marry a man like Hosea, but he was only marrying her because God told him to. It had to have hurt her feelings some."

"I worried that I wasn't being romantic enough," he said as he waited for a car to pass him before he moved into the left lane.

"No, that's not it. And it doesn't really bother me because it's like what you said. I'm glad that you're following the Lord. I want to be married to someone like that. It's just... The idea that someone is marrying me because they have to, instead of because they want to, is a little...hurtful."

"I guess that's the reason you're marrying me though, isn't it?"

She hadn't thought about it that way. That he might feel bad because she couldn't find anyone better to marry her. That she was just desperate enough to take the first marriage proposal that came along and it happened to come from him.

"I'm sorry. I never considered that you might feel the same."

"It doesn't really bother me, because I asked. I wanted you to, I would have felt bad had you said no, but I wasn't deluded into thinking that you said yes because of anything special about me."

"Well, that's not entirely true. If you were not a Christian, I would have said no. And that's final."

"Good to know. But still, we don't really know each other that well. So it wasn't like you chose me. You know?"

"True. I understand what you're saying. And I agree. I guess we can complain about that, but it seems silly to."

"I agree. Is that one of those things that the younger you might have been upset about, but the older you is too pragmatic to even be bothered by?"

"Yes. Exactly. I've grown up. And I think it's mostly a good thing. Although, I guess I wish I could get my excitement about life back. You know?"

"The idea that there's so much ahead of you and you're looking forward to it?"

"That."

"I have that. I'm looking forward to life with you. I'm looking forward to the challenge. This morning was...challenging. And I think that's the way life is going to be for a while. Actually, it will be that way for a long time if we decide that we aren't using birth control. Which is...kind of radical. But Jesus was radical. So I don't think that radical should scare me as long as it's biblical. Something that's not biblical should be the scary thing."

"I agree. But being radical in today's world is to have the rest of society look at you like you're an idiot and treat you like you're stupid. It's definitely something that's going to get you looked down upon."

"That shouldn't bother us. If we're doing what God wants us to do, it doesn't matter what men think about us."

She was quiet, because he was right. But maybe he didn't understand how much pressure there was to conform. She didn't know how many times she'd heard people say that she shouldn't have had so many children, then she wouldn't be in such a pickle when her husband left. Like having her husband leave was something she should have known was going to happen, and having so many children was a mistake.

"Do you have a lot of great memories about Christmas from when you were a child?" she asked, turning the question around back on him and moving the conversation away from birth control. That probably wasn't the best thing for two people who didn't know each other to be talking about. Although, two people who were on their way to get a marriage certificate should have already hashed that out.

She couldn't win.

"I do. My mom is the best cook in the world, and we always had good food to eat. Dad would have more time off from work around the holidays, so we'd get to see him more, and while we probably didn't get as many gifts as most kids our age, I remember there being big piles of presents, that felt like so much, and I always felt spoiled and happy and excited on Christmas."

"Do you remember the day that you realized Santa Claus wasn't real?" she asked, knowing that that was something that had clouded her childhood.

"Mom never did Santa Claus. It just wasn't something that was in the Bible, and I guess she felt like it took away from Christmas or something. Plus, Mom never lied to us. Not once. She might not have told us things, I'm sure there was plenty she didn't tell us, but she never lied to us. Including about Santa Claus."

"I think that's the way to go," she said simply. She hadn't told her kids yes or no about Santa. Other people would ask them if he had come, but she didn't try to hide things from them. She wasn't sure exactly what they believed, and she hadn't tried to convince them either way. "I suppose a parent should guide their children, rather than just letting the chips fall where they would."

"Why do you say that?" he asked as he pulled into the parking lot of the courthouse.

"Because I hadn't really told my kids yes or no about Santa. I just allow it to ride. And when they would ask if Santa Claus would come, I would say, 'what do you think?'"

"That's a nonanswer."

"Yeah. I'm the mom. I should be teaching them, not just allowing them to learn from whatever."

"Well, you can start from today making a new way forward."

"That's what I plan to do."

Today felt like a new beginning almost. Not just about Santa Claus, but about the rest of her life. She had told him she wasn't excited about it anymore, but that wasn't entirely true. She had a little bit more of a realistic view. She knew the work involved, how tired she would be. How hard things could be sometimes, getting to know someone new and bringing that man into her family... It made her nervous, but if she were being honest, she was excited as well. Just...tempered excitement.

He put the truck in park and turned the motor off.

Looking over at her, he said, "Are you ready?"

"I am," she said, with as much confidence as she could put into the words. She was ready. There was no doubt in her mind that she was making a good decision.

Chapter Nine

"Come on in," Pastor Connelly said as he opened the door to his study and stepped back.

Wilson smiled at Charity and allowed her to walk in first.

She gave him a small smile and walked to one of the two chairs that were in front of the pastor's desk where he indicated they could sit.

Wilson closed the door and followed her.

Getting the license had been uneventful, and Wilson was ready to go eat. His stomach was rumbling, and it had already been a big day. He wasn't used to this much excitement. The idea that Charity didn't think birth control was biblical had been a shocker to him. He didn't necessarily agree with her, but he couldn't think of any verses off the top of his head to argue for his position. If the Bible indicated that birth control was something that people shouldn't do, he needed to get on board with it, but there was no prohibition against it, of course.

But like Charity said, God believed that children were a reward. And also, if he was trusting God with his life, shouldn't He trust God with his family size? Wouldn't God know how many children to give him? What made him think that he knew better than God?

He had never considered those things before.

"It's good to see you two today. Thanks for coming on such short notice."

"I appreciate you being willing to marry us on Christmas."

"I think Christmas is a perfect day to get married. Although I don't want to take away from the celebration of Jesus, it is definitely a day to celebrate, and marriage is a reason to celebrate."

"It sure is," he agreed easily as Charity nodded.

"Charity, you'll have to excuse me for a moment while I speak with Wilson about a prior conversation that we had. He admitted that the two of you were getting married, and he called it a marriage of convenience, I believe, without being 'in love.'" The pastor used finger quotes for that. "And he told me that he didn't find it in the Bible that a couple needed to be in love. I find myself agreeing with him, except the Bible does command us to love. We just don't have more than one word for love in our English language, and I believe what most people consider to be 'in love' is actually in lust, or in attraction maybe."

The pastor raised his brows and looked between the two of them.

Wilson nodded, and Charity did as well. He knew the difference between love and lust, and while he had never said "in attraction," he understood that those were feelings that faded over time. And people should never invest and make plans for the rest of their lives because of the way they felt. That changed.

"I did want to make sure that I pointed out that the Bible does command husbands to love their wives. Now, it's a different kind of love than what we think about when we say we're in love."

Wilson nodded; he knew that.

"So we go to first Corinthians 13, which tells us what true love is. 'Charity suffereth long, and is kind; charity envieth not; charity vaunteth not itself, is not puffed up, Doth not behave itself unseemly, seeketh not her own, is not easily provoked, thinketh no evil; Rejoiceth not in iniquity, but rejoiceth in the truth; Beareth all things, believeth all things, hopeth all things, endureth all things. Charity never faileth…'

"We often hear that at weddings, and rightly so, because I don't think that people often realize that love is more than gushy-gushy feelings. There has to be actions—you are kind, you forgive, you are humble, humility may mean accepting less than what you know you deserve, giving up your rights to someone else. That's probably one of the biggest problems in marriage. Each person is determined to make sure that they get what they deserve." The pastor paused. "Humility is whenever you know you deserve more, or the other person deserves less, and yet you give up for them. You make sure that you put yourself under them, delivering, giving more than what you need to, sometimes giving everything."

Wilson sat silent. That kind of thing was not easy. Maybe humility was also admitting that he was wrong or not rubbing it in when he was right. Definitely humility was something that he struggled with, and he figured everyone probably did.

"So the Bible says that love is not proud. You need to remember if you love your wife, you must be humble toward her. You won't rub it in when she's wrong or make sure that she knows that you're better in a certain way. It also means putting her first, because a humble person doesn't need to be first. That, and kindness, will go a long way toward making a marriage great. So, while I agreed with our discussion that you said that maybe people didn't need to be in love in order to get married, I do think that people need to promise to love, but to love in the biblical sense, in order for marriage to be great."

The pastor looked at him, so he said, "I agree. I also agree that it's not going to be easy. I don't think that anyone finds it easy, or marriage wouldn't be such a struggle."

"The Bible says it's a picture of the relationship between Christ and the church. I think maybe that will be a good thing to keep in mind as well. The church doesn't think that they can have authority over Christ, and the wife ought not to think that she can have authority over her husband. I know that's not so popular in many circles, but it's right here in this verse."

Pastor Connelly was quiet for a moment, and Wilson resisted the urge to squirm.

"But, in tandem with that, when you think about how much Christ gave for the church, he gave himself, his very life for the church, he loved it that much. The husband actually has an almost impossible task set before him. To love his wife the way Christ loved the church and gave himself for it. So yes, it's true that the wife is not to usurp authority over the man, and there are no stipulations on that. I know that modern-day people would have it to be so, but there just aren't. But that's why it's important for a woman to choose wisely when she chooses a husband." The pastor smiled at Charity. "And just in case you're wondering, I feel like you've chosen wisely. I've known Wilson for many years now, and I've found him to be an upright man who wants to please the Lord. If there is anyone who will treat you the way Christ has treated the church, Wilson will. Of course, I can't guarantee the way the future will go. Sometimes people who are good decide they don't want to be good anymore. Sometimes people fall away. That's just the way human nature is. And there are no guarantees."

That was a little depressing, and Wilson didn't exactly enjoy hearing it, although it was true. Absolutely true. No one could determine what would happen in the future, only God knew that. Even a person couldn't say for sure whether or not they would fall away. Whether they would stop following the Lord and decide to live for themselves. It was sad, but true.

"All right. I don't want to take any more of your time. I know both of you are busy, and I understand you're heading out to lunch, which is probably a rare occurrence for you, Miss Charity." The pastor smiled benevolently at her.

"It is. I can't remember the last time I went out to eat. I'm really looking forward to it."

Wilson was so glad he had suggested it. She actually did look excited and happy. Maybe relieved, now that some of the burden for everything that had been going on in her life was taken off her shoulders. Maybe it was just his imagination, but he thought she looked younger. Definitely more carefree. It made him happy that he had been able to do that, but his role was far, far from over. He was taking on the biggest challenge of his life, and it wasn't just him who was involved, there were six other souls who would be looking to him to provide and protect and to be the man of God that they deserved to have in their lives.

He couldn't think about that too long, because the responsibility was almost overwhelming. But where God called, He equipped, and he had to believe that.

It wasn't too long before they shook hands with the pastor and made their way out of the study. One of Wilson's goals was to get to know Charity and to develop a relationship with her. He didn't know if falling in love was something that would happen between them, and he supposed he didn't really care. He wanted...wanted a relationship built on mutual respect and admiration. And love. The biblical kind.

Chapter Ten

"That wasn't as bad as I thought it was going to be," Charity said as they walked out of the pastor's house and turned right toward one of the many restaurants in town.

"Yeah, it could have been a lot worse. Like longer. Did you hear my stomach growling?"

Charity laughed and shook her head. "No. It was? I must have been too nervous to pay attention."

"Yeah. I tried to suck it in to stop it, but that's not exactly something you can shush. It wasn't like I yawned."

"No. A yawn probably would have been worse," she said, appreciating the fact that Wilson was so easy to talk to.

"Do you have a preference about which restaurant you'd like to eat at?"

"I was serious when I told Pastor Connelly that I haven't eaten out in years, maybe even a decade. I'll go anywhere that will cook my food for me, serve it, and clean up after me."

"All right. Then let's go here. Maybe because it's first and fastest," Wilson said, again causing her to laugh. She appreciated his humor more than she could say. Definitely with the life that she led, a person had to have a sense of humor, otherwise it would be almost unimaginably bleak.

They went in and were seated right away at a cute little table near the window.

"Goodness. It's been so long since I've been in a restaurant, I just feel like I need to sit here and enjoy it for a minute," she said as she put her hand on the menu, just imagining all the good food that was in there waiting to be cooked just for her. When was the last time somebody made something for her to eat and she didn't have to do it herself? Or cleaned up after her? Normally she didn't just cook for herself but for her kids, and she cleaned up after everyone as well.

"I didn't realize something this simple would make you so happy," he said, smiling at her.

She was a little embarrassed because she was acting like a child, getting so excited about eating out. But it was a big deal to her. "I'm sorry. I'll try to be a little bit more mature."

"No. It's fine. I'm enjoying watching you."

She smiled but tried to curtail her enthusiasm. She opened her menu and looked for something she couldn't make at home herself.

The waitress came and took their orders, and maybe there was a little bit of surprise on her face to see the two of them together, but there was no comment.

That was something Charity was a little nervous about. The townspeople would see that there was a huge discrepancy between herself and Wilson. Wilson was successful and well respected, well-off, and a pillar of the community. She, on the other hand, was the wife that her husband didn't want, left saddled with five children, and she was barely keeping her head above water, and in fact she was on the verge of losing not just her house but her kids too. She was hardly a respected pillar of the community, although she did have her integrity intact. She wasn't the one who cheated, she wasn't the one who broke up her family, and she wasn't the one who caused it, although her husband had blamed her. That hardly seemed fair, but she didn't want to think about that now.

"So, tell me about you? You're a farmer. Is there something else you do too?" she asked as the waitress left to get their drinks.

"Well, I started a business in college. It was a cleaning company that morphed into a handyman-type thing. It grew, and grew, and grew some more, and eventually I hired people to run it, went public with it, selling the stock on the open market, and I make a tidy little profit on it, without the headache of managing it."

"I see. Wow. So you do that in addition to farming?"

"There's really nothing for me to do. It's just a company that I own the majority of the shares in and makes a nice profit every year, and I don't have to lift a finger. Plus, I have the money I sold it for, but I mostly used that to buy the farm."

"It's neat that you came back here to Mistletoe Meadows. You must really love it here."

"I do. No doubt about it. But this is where my family is. I probably would have come back anyway, just because I wanted to be around them. That's one thing I learned when I went to school. You can't replace your family. And I wouldn't want to."

"I wonder if that's because you had so many siblings? Do you think larger families tend to be closer?"

"Maybe. Are you not close with your family?"

"I barely talk to my older sister. I'll probably get a card from her here today or tomorrow, and she may call on my birthday. Otherwise... There's no contact."

"What about your parents?"

"Same. They go scuba diving in the Caribbean on Thanksgiving. So obviously we don't have a family Thanksgiving dinner, and this year for Christmas, they're spending it in Jamaica. I guess it's nice and warm down there. So yeah. I'll probably talk some when they get back, but it's not going to be a close family Christmas or anything."

"What about their grandkids? Don't they want to see them?"

"I'm not sure they can even tell you their names."

"I need to learn their names. I know you told me the little dude I was holding was Evans, but there are four other ones, and I need to figure those out too."

"Well, I can run them through for you, but I don't expect you to learn them all at once in like two minutes. I had them over eight years, so it's a little bit different."

"But I want to."

That made her heart smile. That he thought that her children were important. And learning their names was a priority for him.

"I really wanted to know about you." She felt like she talked nonstop. He figured out her views on birth control, which was a rather private thing, before they barely even knew each other, and she hadn't even known what his job was until just now. Definitely she'd been talking too much.

"All right, I'll tell you what. I'll ask a question and you answer it, then you get to ask a question and I'll answer it. Is that a good deal?"

She loved that he tried to make things fair. Not that everything could always be fair, but it was nice that he gave a nod to her concern. It made her feel seen and valued. "That sounds fine."

"All right. I answered your question about what I did, in addition to farming. I guess I could tell you some about my farm. I have beef cattle, and I make hay for them to eat over the winter. I don't grow corn, although sometimes I'll buy it, if I don't feel like I have enough hay to make it through. I grow some vegetables and sell some of that stuff, but that's a lot more labor intensive, and I've veered away from that over the years."

"Sounds like a dream," she said, meaning it. She would love to grow all of her own food, although... The work involved made her rethink that idea. Going to the grocery store was so much easier than weeding in the garden then harvesting then putting it up. Then she had to figure out her meals based on what was already in the freezer.

"Is it my turn?" he asked, seeming to watch her as she thought about things.

"Of course. I'm sorry. I was just thinking about how much I would love to grow my own food, but then I thought about how much work it was, and…maybe going to the grocery store isn't so bad."

"Well, you have five kids. You don't need to take on more work. And here's a question. Tell me their names and ages if I can do that in one question."

She laughed. "We're not keeping score. I can tell you their names and ages."

"All right. I'm listening, or maybe I should take notes."

"I'll tell you as many times as you need me to. I don't expect you to remember it the first time you're told." She certainly had trouble with other people's kids' names, so she could understand the issue. To her, it was easy, but everyone said the kids all looked alike.

"Gifford's the oldest, he's eight. He is the one that probably has had the hardest time with his dad leaving, other than Banks. He's really struggled too. He's five."

"Gifford and Banks. Gotcha. Struggling with their dad. I think five is a really bad age."

"Yeah. I probably could have sent him to kindergarten this year, but with all the other changes in our life, I just felt like it might have been too much."

"That's probably a wise decision, although I feel like it's better to graduate early than late. You only have so much of your life to live, and you don't want to waste it on school."

"No. But it is nice to be able to stay home. You have an extra year with your family and an extra year to get grounded in what you believe."

"That's a good point."

"Lavinia is four. She was the one with all the playdough. She's very artistic and particular about what color she gets. I only let them play with one color at a time, otherwise we would have a great big glob of dark gray playdough. I know that's mean, but I'm a mean mom."

"That's not mean, that's wise, and good for you for sticking to your guns."

It was nice to hear someone say that she was doing something right. It was hard not to just stop there and smile for a little bit.

"The two youngest are Serafina, who's two, and then Evans, who's one."

"All of your kids are pretty close together. That was eight, five and four, then two and one."

"Yeah, Gifford just turned eight at the end of August, and Banks turned five just after the cutoff for kindergarten. That's the biggest gap."

He seemed thoughtful, and she debated about asking him why. Finally, she decided that she was going to be married to him, she couldn't be afraid to ask him questions.

"Does it bother you that they're so close together?"

"I guess I was just thinking about birth control and how many children we might end up having if it's not a thing, but... If I trust God, it shouldn't matter. I hate to say that though, because there's a lot of people who use birth control, and they consider themselves Christians who trust God as well. I just...think that it might be wise to pray about that some more."

"That's fine." He was thinking about it. That was all she needed to see. If he made a decision against it, it would be fine, and if he was supporting her and what she believed, that would be just as well also. She gave him a thoughtful glance.

"You know whatever you decide will be okay with me?"

"Really?"

"Yes. I mean, I don't really want to be forced to take birth control that I feel is causing a fertilized egg to not implant, because I don't feel like that's right. I know that happens at times, that an egg naturally gets fertilized and just doesn't implant for whatever reason, but I don't want to do that chemically on purpose."

"Gotcha. I agree with you on that. That's a definite no for us."

Chapter Eleven

Charity nodded, grateful that Wilson saw that her way and wondering how she would have handled it if he hadn't. It probably didn't matter, since there were multiple different kinds of birth control, and she didn't have to choose one that went against her beliefs.

"So, what's your favorite color?" He grinned at her.

She waited while the waitress came back, setting their drinks down before walking away again. "Purple. It's a color you can use with boys or girls, and it just looks happy to me. And it makes me feel calm."

"If I hadn't been at your house this morning, I might not have realized what a gift calmness is, so maybe we should paint the entire house purple."

"I think that's a great idea. Although, I think sometimes when you get too much of something, you get sick of it."

"I don't think I'll ever get sick of my favorite color."

"I'd like to ask you what it is, but I thought of a different question that I really want to know the answer to."

"She doesn't want to know what my favorite color is?" He looked up at the sky like he was talking to the Lord. "I don't think she likes me all that much."

"What's your favorite color?" she capitulated.

"It's blue. Like all good men, I love the color blue. And since you asked me the question I wanted you to ask me, now you can ask your question."

She wasn't going to argue with getting an extra turn, so she jumped right into her question. "Where are we going to live?"

She tried not to hold her breath. After all, he hadn't even said that they were going to live together. She just assumed. He had gone on all of that discussion about how important families were and all that stuff, and for some reason, she just figured that he would be moving in. But it was an assumption, and she could be wrong.

"Well, I guess that's something we'll have to talk about. I do believe that the man should be the head of the home. The Bible says so, but that doesn't mean that the man's the only one making the decisions and the woman just has to sit there and do whatever he says."

"That's nice to hear," she said, but she figured that it might be harder to live out. Clancy hadn't been a very good Christian and often browbeat her with the fact that she was supposed to submit to him. It was funny that he never, even one time, admitted that he didn't treat her the way he was supposed to or the way he was commanded to in the Bible, to give himself for her the way Christ gave himself for the church. Interesting that he picked and chose what parts of the Bible he wanted to browbeat her with.

"I hoped that we could sell your house and move into mine. It would give us a little bit of wiggle room, financially, not that we have to count our pennies, because we can afford both houses, but I think the kids would really enjoy living on the farm, and it might be a place that you could make use of too. If you are doing your baking and want to expand it, there's already an outbuilding for that very thing."

"You're kidding," she said, shocked. It was like God had just set the desire of her heart right down in her lap. She had always wanted to be able to open up her own baking business and turn it into something profitable, but she was limited in what she could do out of her kitchen in her house.

"Nope. I'm serious. But I don't want to make you move out of your house if you don't want to. This isn't something that I am unwilling to negotiate on. We can talk about it."

"Well, on the one hand, I know that it would be better for the children to have stability, but on the other, growing up on a farm is probably the absolute best place that you could raise children. And I know that they would love it. Plus, you're right about us not needing to pay for two houses. And the money that we would make selling that house would be beneficial, although... I might have to split it with Clancy. I'll have to look into that."

"Maybe you can let me know what the terms of your divorce are?"

She hated that word. The D word. The word she never said, the word she cried over when her husband had said it to her. It was the one thing she didn't want to have happen to her in her life. Cancer would have been preferable to divorce. Sad, but true.

"Yes, absolutely. I have sole custody of the children. He wasn't interested. And he didn't want any of the house, but we didn't have it put in my name, so it's in both of our names. That's why I'm not sure how it will go when we sell it. But he basically walked away from everything and told me he wouldn't fight for anything as long as I didn't insist that he had to pay child support."

"What?" Wilson said, which was the reaction of pretty much everyone that she had ever said that to. She wasn't sure why she said it so freely. She should have been more cautious. "He's not paying child support?"

"First of all, he's in Australia, so it would be kind of hard for the United States government to force him to do that. And secondly, I didn't want any strings attached. So, I gave him whatever he wanted, but I wouldn't budge on the children. They are mine, solely mine."

"I see." It might have been her imagination, but it looked like admiration that entered his eyes. "Wow. That was...courageous."

"Or stupid. Most people say stupid." She nodded, narrowing her eyes and just being honest. That was pretty much the conclusion of everyone she talked to. They didn't understand how important her children were to her. She didn't want them to be brought up in a home where they were taught that it was okay to commit adultery, to sleep with another woman's husband, to leave your five children and run off just because you claim that you are in love.

All those things that Clancy and his girlfriend could teach her children. She wanted them away from that influence. And Clancy didn't have any interest in being a father in their lives. So it wasn't like she needed to worry about it anyway.

"I would have been okay if he wanted to see his children. I wouldn't have kept them from him, but he wasn't interested in that. He just wanted to not have to pay so much child support, so he was going to insist on half custody. When I gave up the idea of child support, he was totally willing to give up all rights to custody. It was that easy."

"It was about money, rather than the things that were really important, your children."

"Yes." She nodded, grateful that Wilson understood. He truly got it and knew why she couldn't do what everyone thought she should have done and fought for child support.

"You chose the harder way, in order to do the better thing for your children."

"That's right." Their eyes met, and she felt like something stirred between them. Something real and...visceral. Her fingers started to tingle. She was suddenly very aware of where he was across from her, and for some reason, she wanted to move closer, to move her hand so it touched his, like she needed that physical contact.

She didn't know how long they stared at each other. It was

probably only a few seconds before the waitress came with their orders, setting a plate down in front of her and one down in front of him.

After saying they should let her know if they needed anything, she walked away. The spell was broken. Although, the feeling remained. The feeling that...she liked Wilson. Truly liked him, not just as a person, but...as a man.

She wasn't under any illusions that he felt the same about her though. After all, she was a lot different than he was. She could go through all the ways that she was inferior, but she didn't want to depress herself.

Instead, she looked at her food and closed her eyes, breathing in the aroma and feeling totally spoiled and coddled at the food that she had not had to prepare, that was sitting in front of her ready to eat.

"Shall I pray?" Wilson asked as she opened her eyes.

"Sure," she said, smiling and closing her eyes again. She listened to his deep voice rumble across the table. She did still have some misgivings, mostly related to what people were going to think when they found out golden boy Wilson McBride had taken up with her, scourge of the town. Although that might be overestimating it just slightly, people were going to talk. They were going to say that she did something to catch him, to snare him, because she didn't think that any of them would believe that he wanted her for her.

And that wasn't true anyway. He didn't want her for her, he was here because he felt it was the will of the Lord.

"Aren't you going to eat?" he asked, already having a bite of food on his fork and having it lifted halfway to his mouth.

"I just want to savor the moment. This is so nice."

"We'll have to go out at least once a week. You know, date night and all of that."

"I don't even know what date night is anymore."

"Well, I've always thought that a man should court his wife before their marriage and date her afterward, but... I wasn't expecting to marry a woman with five children. It might be kind of hard to get away from them."

"The hard thing is finding someone who's willing to watch them. That's never easy."

"I see. Thanks for the warning. I guess I should start lining people up."

"You do that. Let me know how it works out for you. Typically, people run the other direction when they find out that I want them to watch my children. It's not that the kids are so bad, it's that there's five of them."

He laughed as she stuck the first bite of her meal in her mouth and closed her eyes, trying not to sigh out loud. "We're definitely having date nights. At least until you can eat without closing your eyes and making groaning sounds."

"I did not groan."

"I heard you."

"You're making that up."

"I'll record it next time and play it back to you. In fact, I can use it as blackmail."

"Fine. I'll stop groaning."

"Actually, you should keep groaning, because I'll take you out as long as you keep doing it."

"Just so you can make fun of me?"

"You're so cute when your cheeks get red, and your nose turns pink, and you get that self-conscious smile on your face because you know I'm right."

"I know no such thing. My hearing is getting bad, because I'm getting older, but I would definitely hear myself groan, and I did not, so I maintain that I did not groan."

He put food in his mouth and just gave her a superior look. It was fake, and cute, and she giggled. He was so much fun. Funny and charming and thoughtful and considerate... Perfect. He was perfect. She had no idea what the man was doing with her.

"Wilson McBride. Look at you over here in the corner by yourself."

Charity looked up to see Beth Gibson walking toward them.

Not that Beth was looking at Charity. Not at all. Her eyes were fixed on Wilson. And Charity couldn't blame her. Wilson was quite good-looking, and she wouldn't stop looking at him if it wouldn't make things so awkward.

"Aren't you going to take another bite?" Wilson asked, and she wasn't sure he even had turned his head.

"I am. I want to make it last though."

"Wilson? Did you hear me?" Beth stopped at their table and leaned down on it. Her shirt was rather low, and there was a good bit of cleavage that spilled out.

Charity looked up, saw the cleavage, blinked, and looked back down quickly at her plate, embarrassed.

She couldn't imagine wearing something so revealing. Mostly because it was not modest, and the Bible commanded Christians to be modest, but also because...it was just so weird, the idea that a person would show their private areas to anyone who cared to look.

"It's a nice day, Beth. Thanks for stopping by, but I'm with my fiancée, and we're on a tight schedule, so if you don't mind," Wilson said, causing Charity to look up. Really? His fiancée? She supposed she was, but she didn't have a ring.

"I don't see a ring. Fiancée? Why haven't I heard about that?"

"It just happened, and even though I didn't have a ring, she agreed to marry me anyway." Wilson's words were smooth.

"What's she doing with you? Is there something she's blackmailing you over? I mean, come on, this is Charity Ames. She's got five kids. She's the one whose husband ditched her, couldn't stand her, and ran off with that woman who was butt ugly, because he was so desperate to get away from her. I heard he fled the country and is living in Austria or something."

It was Australia, but Charity wasn't going to correct her. She just said all the things Charity thought in her mind to herself. She wasn't worthy of Wilson.

"You know, it's funny, because I was wondering what she is doing with a man like me. Someone as talented and amazing as Charity is. She's challenged my views on the Bible, giving verses to back up her position, and I really love having intellectual conversations where the woman I'm talking to doesn't just agree with everything I say but has opinions of her own. Her intelligence is really what I fell in love with to begin with."

Now he was making it up. Because he hadn't fallen in love. They'd talked about that. They didn't believe in it. And yet here he was telling Beth that's what happened.

Charity was a little annoyed at that, and maybe Wilson saw her face. Because his hand descended on hers, and he squeezed until she looked up at him.

"Are you okay?"

"I am." It was true. He was being so solicitous and sweet. How could she not be okay?

"So you're saying Charity is smart? She didn't even go to college. She got married right away and started popping out babies."

"I guess I don't think that going to college makes you smart. I spent some time in school with people who didn't know a whole lot but were there because Mommy and Daddy wanted them there. I guess I would rather be with someone who knew what she wanted and went after it and wasn't afraid to not do what everyone else was doing."

That was her, that was for sure, Charity thought to herself.

"Well, I am going to be spreading this all around town. I don't think anyone knows that Wilson McBride is now a taken man. Of course, engagements don't always last, do they?" Beth said, looking at Charity. "Just like marriages don't always last. A woman's husband might leave her for someone uglier and worse than she is, just to get away from her."

Beth wrinkled her nose and straightened up from the table.

"I'll leave you two to your meal. Since you're on a tight schedule." She said that in a rather nasty way before putting her nose in the air and walking away.

Charity wanted to cry. Everything that Beth said was true. Absolutely true, and it was what the entire town said and thought about her. And yet Wilson wanted to marry her. Maybe he didn't understand how badly everyone thought about her. It was up to her to let him know.

Chapter Twelve

What Beth Gibson had done, the way she had insulted and belittled Charity, could have ruined the rest of the meal. Wilson would have allowed it to ruin his. But he hadn't counted on Charity.

It had upset her, of that he was sure, but after Beth left, she put another bite in her mouth, swallowed, and then looked at him. "She's right. All that stuff is true."

"It wasn't nice," he said. It didn't matter whether it was true or not. Of course he didn't want people going around telling lies, but just because something was true didn't mean it had to come out of a person's mouth.

"But it's good that she did that. I... You should know what you're getting into."

"I know what I'm getting into. And I meant every word I said."

"You said you were falling in love with me. That wasn't true."

"How do you know?" he asked, and there was a little smile on his mouth. Because... He had felt something earlier, he didn't even remember what they were talking about, but it was like the whole world went on without them. It was just the two of them, and he never felt like that with anyone before. He wanted to move his fingers over, touch her, feel connected to her amidst all the other things that were happening around them, and know that the two of them, in the universe, were together. It was an odd sensation.

"Because we only started talking today. And—"

"You're my fiancée. We're getting married."

"We just decided that today. You can't possibly be falling in love with me?"

"People say there's such a thing as love at first sight. Why couldn't there be such a thing as love at first proposal or something?"

"The fact of the matter is not everything you said was true."

"When and how I fall in love is up to me. And I choose to say that I'm falling in love with you. I'm going to love you for the rest of my life. And that's just the way it's going to be."

It seemed simple to him. His feelings were under his control. He was not under their control. So many times, people got it backward, even him. Sometimes he allowed his feelings to control him, but not with this. Not with something so important. Plus, there was that moment they shared. If he were a contemplative sort, he would want to think about that for a while. But it was enough that they had it, and he thought, was almost sure, that there would be more moments just like that.

"All right. I'll give you that. Still, be warned. You can't say you didn't know. And if you need to back out, I understand. It's fine."

"Same for you. You can back out too, if you want to. As for me, I made up my mind before I even went to your house. It wouldn't matter what anyone said. I know what God wants me to do, and I'm going to do it, and I'm going to love you, and I'm going to stay married to you for the rest of my life. Unless you choose otherwise." He grinned a little. "Which I hope you don't."

She laughed and shook her head. "All right. If that's how you feel about it, and you're not going to allow a comment like that bother you, then I'm not going to let Beth bother me either. She's right, and I wish it weren't true, but it's behind me. The rest of my life is ahead of me, and I'm going to change and walk a different way."

"Hopefully not too different. Because I like you the way you are."

"No. Just different in the eyes of the town. I'm going to marry someone who's going to stay with me, for one."

"Oh. I like that. Okay, well, in that case, I'm all for it. Because I don't want anyone to think that I'm the same as Clancy."

"Oh, goodness, no. You two are as different as night and day, with you being all the good things and him being...everything I don't want."

He looked at her gently as she looked down at her food, like she was thinking.

"I was really stupid at one point in my life. I sure hope I don't have that problem again."

"I think we gain wisdom as we age; that's one of the benefits of aging. There are a lot of downsides," he said, and that caused her to laugh.

"Tell me about it. I'm not even that old, and I can see that it only goes downhill from here."

"Some things, some things actually get better. Like wisdom. But only if we allow it deliberately. Some people absolutely refuse to allow themselves to get smarter."

"Or admit that they need to get smarter. I think that's probably the first problem that many of us have. We just don't want to admit that there are things that we don't know, things that we can learn, even from people we don't like."

"Now that's a good point. And absolutely true." He took a breath. "I think that is the pride the pastor was talking about. How we have a tendency to think we're right and not want to hear anyone else's side of the story. We do that in marriages, and friendships, and in our daily lives."

"Exactly. And I think it's something that we can guard against if we know we do it."

"Can I get you two anything else? Dessert?" the waitress said as she stopped at their table, setting the bill down and picking up their empty plates.

"I'm so full I couldn't eat another thing," Charity said, smiling and looking pleased. It made his heart happy to see how happy a simple meal made her. It didn't cost much, and it was just the diner in town, but she acted like he'd given her so much more. It was nice to be with someone who was grateful.

He wasn't sure that he'd ever been with anyone who really appreciated what he had done for them, and not that he had done a whole lot. Hopefully he'd grown since those days when he expected to be appreciated, but he didn't recall anyone ever appreciating him the way Charity did. It was a refreshing change.

He handed the waitress a card along with the bill, and she walked away with their empty plates, murmuring that she'd be right back.

"We don't have to go straight home if you don't want to. Mom hasn't sent me any SOS's unless she's sent you one that I don't know about."

"I would have said something right away. But nobody wants me, and that's always a good thing when you have small children," she said, holding up her phone which showed a picture of her kids in the background and no messages on her screen.

"Well then, we're free to continue if you'd like."

"I think we better get back. We don't want to wear your mom out on her very first day with the kids. It would be nice if she would agree to do it at least once more before she gets scared away."

"I think you'll be surprised. Mom will have the kids well in hand when we get home, and she might not even let us in, because she won't want to give them up."

"Well, that vision is completely opposite of what I'm afraid of, which is my kids will have the house completely trashed with your mom tied up in a closet somewhere."

He laughed. "Give Mom some credit. She did raise six kids."

"I know. I guess in most situations, I'm all about positive thinking and all that, but in this instance, I think that maybe it might be best to be prepared for the worst."

"All right. You have your vision, I have mine. Mostly because I have faith in my mom. I kinda think that's the kind of grandma you're going to be."

She laughed again. "I can't even imagine being a grandma at this point. The idea of my little kids growing up and having children of their own is just so...foreign, but wonderful at the same time."

He laughed. "Wonderful because they're not yours to take care of anymore?"

"Maybe. Or maybe because they've grown up into people who love God and serve Him. That's my only goal. Really. Other than teaching them to read and write and do a little bit of math."

"That's probably all we need. Although, I think the school district would like to see them do some more."

"I have very low standards, I guess, because in that area, I feel like they can teach themselves everything they really want to, but they might not teach themselves about the Lord, that's my job."

"And mine," he said as the waitress brought his receipt back, and he signed it before they stood together.

"Thank you very much. That was...the best time I've had in a long time."

"Hopefully there will be a lot more times like that in your future. Although, you're probably going to get tired of me."

"I don't think so. I guess I could be wrong, but I kinda feel like you're the kind of person that I'll always be interested in. You're always going to have something interesting to say."

"I'll try. But we might end up being like other married couples who talk about bills and diapers and household repairs."

"I guess I won't mind that." She sighed.

"Just because there's someone to talk about those things with you?" he asked, and while he was only partially teasing, he was also serious, because that was almost certainly a problem. She didn't have anyone to talk about those things with.

"Yeah. It won't be all on my shoulders anymore. Speaking of, I'm totally fine with moving out of my house into yours and selling mine. How soon were you thinking to do that?"

"Well, if we get married on Christmas—?" He kind of let the sentence trail off as though he were asking her.

"That's fine with me. I mean, if you're willing to do it that quickly, I'm certainly not going to stand in your way."

"I want to do it that quickly. Not that I'm willing. Which I am."

She smiled at his insistence. Somehow, he felt like it was really important to let her know that this was what he wanted. Sure, he was following what God wanted him to do, but the more he talked to Charity, the more he was sure that God knew exactly what He was doing, not that he ever doubted it. But maybe it would be better for him to say the more he talked to her, the more he wanted to do what God wanted him to do, just because of Charity.

They walked out of the restaurant and moseyed down the street toward his truck.

"So if we get married on Christmas, can we use the week between Christmas and New Year's to move into my house? I don't want to push you, but at the same time, there's no point in dragging our feet."

"I agree. I know that'll be fine. We might as well let the children know that this change is going to include moving to a new home. I... I think they'll be excited about it. Even Gifford, maybe even mostly Gifford, if being on the farm is as fun as I think it's going to be."

"I'll try to make sure that it's fun. And Gifford can help if he wants to. There are plenty of things that an eight-year-old can do, and he'll actually be quite an asset, I think. Although, if it is not something that he's interested in, we don't have to push it."

"Thank you. Thank you for taking that into consideration and also for being willing to talk to me about it. I would have stressed about this, because I probably wouldn't have asked."

"You know you can ask me anything. I hope I can do the same with you."

"But some things are awkward, you know?" She looked up at him, and as he looked down, she seemed to be asking him to understand, so he bit back the automatic reply, which was along the lines of "even if it's hard, we should ask anyway" and tried to think about his words.

"I guess it was hard for me to come to your door this morning. I'm not even sure why. Because I knew I was doing what God wanted me to do, even if you said no, but that was what I was nervous about. That you were going to laugh at me and slam the door in my face."

"Nobody wants that. But... First of all, I didn't answer the door, so you worried needlessly." They laughed together. "And secondly, I don't think I've ever laughed in someone's face or delighted in a rejection. If I had to reject someone, I would want to do it easily, gently, without hurting their feelings any more than I had to. I mean, I want to treat them the way I would want to be treated."

"Yeah. Do unto others as you would have them do unto you, even when you're rejecting them and telling them to buzz off."

"Yeah. Just like that." They laughed together, because both of them knew that neither one of them would tell the other to buzz off.

"All right then, we just agreed to talk about things, although... I guess sometimes communication is elevated to a biblical standard, and it's not."

"Isn't it funny how we get confused about those things?" she asked as they reached his pickup and he walked around to her side so that he could open the door.

"Yeah. Even Christians start thinking things like communication, which has been preached in secular circles, is the most important thing in marriage, but... The Bible doesn't say that at all. Probably the most important thing will be to treat the other person the way you want to be treated, but God also commands us to be kind and to love, to be gentle, and to let no corrupt communication proceed out of our mouth. All that would be more important than talking about things, at least in my opinion, and that's backed up with Bible."

"Well, we're in agreement on that. The Bible trumps secular 'wisdom.'" He liked the way she said wisdom, like sometimes it really wasn't wisdom after all.

He had to agree with that assessment.

They chatted on the way home, nothing earth-shattering, just getting to know each other, and by the time they reached her house and walked up the sidewalk, he was feeling pretty good about the two of them.

She knew her kids better than he did, and there was a nagging worry in the back of his head that maybe his mother really was tied up in the closet somewhere. He...might be in some trouble for that.

"It's quiet," she said as they stood at the door, her hand on the knob.

"I don't think that's always a good thing when it comes to children?"

"Usually it's not a good thing," she said, narrowing her eyes, and then she tilted her head. "But I hear laughter."

"That's my mom," he said, feeling the swelling deep in his chest, and he knew it was pride because his mom was pretty awesome.

"You love her. That's so sweet." Charity glanced back up at him and then turned the doorknob and pushed it open.

She was right. He did love his mom, and he appreciated the fact that his fiancée, soon to be wife, appreciated that. Some women seemed to be jealous of that bond that a mom might have with her son and worked to destroy it. Those women were foolish. Especially when he was talking about a woman as awesome as his mother. Not that he thought that Charity could learn a thing or two, because he felt like she was pretty amazing as well, but anyone who was open could always learn, and his mother was a good woman to learn from. He knew Charity would be wise in that area. And it was just one more thing that made him feel like his decision was the right one, exactly what God wanted.

"Are you guys home already?" his mom said as they walked in.

"That's not the way people usually greet me after I've left them with my children for an afternoon."

"It's only been two hours. It wasn't a whole afternoon." His mom looked around at all the children who were sitting at the table, cut-up grapes in front of them, and little...it looked like shot glasses of water.

"Are those shot glasses?" Wilson asked, squinting at the glasses and then looking at his mom.

"What do you know about shot glasses, son?" she asked him, her eyes twinkling.

"Nothing," he said, his hands in the air like she was pointing a gun at him.

His mom laughed, and better yet, Charity laughed as well.

"They're little dessert glasses I got somewhere and thought I would never use, and I threw them in my purse today because I thought they would be really great water glasses for little kids, and it turns out that children want water whenever it's in a cute little glass, and I love water when it gets spilled out of that cute little glass because there's not much to clean up."

"I underestimated your mother. You're right. She is awesome. I'm not even sure that word is strong enough to describe her," Charity said as she turned to Wilson and spoke with awe in her voice.

"Pshaw!" his mother said, waving her hand around. "It's just as you get older, you learn a few tricks. Plus, I don't like to throw things away, so the dessert glasses get used, I didn't have to throw them away."

"How did you get them to be so quiet?" Wilson asked, remembering how crazy everything was when they had left that morning.

"We were playing the quiet game."

"The quiet game?" Charity asked.

Wilson just laughed. His mom had played the quiet game with them more than once. Although, he saw a bag of chocolate chips beside her, and he didn't recall that being part of the quiet game growing up.

"Sure. The quiet game. It's a game we play, where everyone has to be quiet, and the first person who talks loses, and everyone else gets a chocolate chip."

"Oh. My. Goodness," Charity said. She turned again to Wilson. "I believe your mother just might qualify for sainthood."

"I'm sure she's already qualified for sainthood, but that is pretty brilliant, if you ask me."

"Same. Oh my goodness, so much the same."

"We had a great time. Next time, you guys can stay out much longer."

It looked like the littlest one was not up from his nap, since he wasn't at the table. Evans. That one was named Evans. But the rest of the kids sat quietly at the table, none of them wanting to speak first and not get a chocolate chip.

"All right, since I suppose it's time for me to leave, I'll give you all two chocolate chips, since all of you were quiet and did not speak and since I have to leave."

"No, don't go!" Banks cried, looking like he was going to cry.

"Oh, don't worry, you're going to be seeing a lot of me, because your mom is marrying my son which makes me your grandmother."

"Grandmother?" Gifford said, squinting his eyes as though he wasn't quite sure exactly what that was. It made Wilson's heart squeeze just a little, that the child didn't know any of his grandparents apparently. He hadn't thought to ask about Clancy's parents, but obviously they weren't swooping in to help Charity in any way.

"Of course, although all my other grandchildren call me Grandma. Which, if that's okay with your mother, will be what you call me too."

"Mom?" Gifford turned to his mother, and she nodded, and there were tears in her eyes.

This family needed love so bad, and it wasn't hard for Wilson to figure out exactly why God had prompted him; they needed him. But more than that, he had a feeling that he needed them, Charity in particular.

"I guess we can talk about what we're doing between now and Christmas, but maybe I can call you tomorrow?" he said as his mother gathered up her things, the children clambering around her, begging her not to go.

"Sure. Let me give you my number," she said, turning to him and blinking, as though she needed to get her bearings again. "I guess I'm getting a husband, and my children are getting a father, and your mom is part of the package deal, and that's a huge gift to us all."

"Be careful, or I'm going to get jealous and start thinking you like her more than you like me."

She laughed, and he was glad to hear that. He'd rather have that than crying any day, although he supposed he was going to have to learn to deal with the tears, he just wasn't sure how. He never really had to before.

She gave him her number, and he programmed it into his phone and then texted her. Her phone buzzed with his text, and he smiled and nodded. "There. You've got my number in case you need it, and I'll call you sometime tomorrow, and maybe we can go to the Christmas Eve service if nothing else together?"

"Sure. And I'll start trying to pack some things up so that we can work on getting moved, although the Secret Saint dropped off a ton of presents for the kids, so there's going to be a lot of packing after Christmas too."

He grinned inside. He had been responsible for making sure that the Secret Saint did not miss Charity's house and children.

"Not a big deal. And you don't have to pack anything. I'll help you, and we can do it together."

"I know that you have to have things you have to do, and packing up my house doesn't need to be one of them."

"I don't mind helping. Although I can't do it tomorrow morning. Maybe I can help you later on?"

"I'll probably pack in the morning and try to be pretty quiet while the kids are taking their naps."

"All right. We'll go back to planning. I'll call you and figure things out from there."

"Sounds good," she said, and he took one last look at her before he opened the door and helped his mother out, a good feeling in his heart.

Chapter Thirteen

he Christmas Eve service was always excellent, and this year was no different.

What was different was the fact that Charity was standing beside Wilson, and even better was the fact that she wanted to and was enjoying it.

She didn't know that standing beside a man, the right man, could make all the difference when a person went to church.

When she was able to get Clancy to go, he complained the whole time, came late, left early, and always wanted to sit in the back.

They were still sitting in the back, because of the children. They didn't want them to interrupt the service for anyone else and didn't want to have to walk halfway through the church if they needed to leave in the middle of it because one of them got antsy. Still, everything else was better. Wilson acted like he enjoyed the entire service, and it seemed like he enjoyed the music just as much as she did. Kyra had given her a special look and a great big smile when she saw that Wilson stood beside her.

She had grinned back, and the communication that had passed between them was happy and joyful.

Charity couldn't deny that she was looking forward to her marriage, even though it was an adjustment, and every once in a while, she had an attack of anxiety. Was she making the right decision? Maybe she shouldn't go through with it. Was she doing the right thing for her children? Was Wilson going to regret it?

That last question was probably the one that haunted her the most.

"I'll never get tired of listening to the string music. So glad we have a trio like that in Mistletoe Meadows." Wilson leaned down and spoke in her ear, and it sent shivers the whole way to her toes. Her two youngest children were in the nursery, and the three oldest had been trained since birth to sit quietly in the service, and they did so now.

It was a peaceful time, coming to church, sometimes the only break she had where she could actually sit and relax.

"Same. This is my favorite service of the entire year."

"Mine too. I love Sunday evening services. They're just always so comfortable, but this one beats everything."

She loved Christmas Eve, loved the anticipation, the excitement, the idea that something special was coming, that God had sent His son, and the whole world rejoiced, the angels celebrated his birth. Even the mother and father gently watching over their child gave her that happy feeling in her stomach. The celebration, the quiet anticipation of Christians across the globe. It was the one time that they were all in tune together.

Of course, she loved the decorations and the sparkle and the lights and the good food and fellowship, just everything.

"Are we staying for refreshments afterward?" Wilson breathed in her ear as the pastor thanked the trio and invited everyone downstairs for refreshments.

"If it's okay with you. I don't know how long the kids will hold out, but I know we'd all love to get something."

"I had my eye on that pie you made."

"I have another one at home. You can have some of that."

"I wasn't sure I was going to get any or not, so I figured I probably ought to grab a piece here while I can."

"You can have the whole thing." She owed him that and so much more. Although she knew if she said that, he would brush her off, saying that she didn't owe him anything and maybe even arguing that he owed her. But that wasn't true. She was definitely the one who was getting the most out of this bargain, and she knew it. And she was grateful.

"All right then, let's stay. And if we need to go, we'll go. You just say the word."

"All right." He had said that he wasn't going to stay overnight tonight, although he had asked for permission to come in the morning and spend Christmas with them. She had gladly given it, of course, and it would have been okay if he had stayed the night. But she didn't tell him that. There wasn't too much she would have denied him at this point, and it wasn't just because she was grateful. It was because he inspired her to want to be better, to want to treat others the way she wanted to be treated because that was how he treated everyone.

Still, they were planning on getting married tomorrow sometime in the afternoon. And then he would be sleeping on her couch until they moved into his farmhouse, he'd already told her that much.

It had taken all the guesswork out of everything, and she appreciated that. She didn't have to wonder what was going to happen and think about whether or not she should ask him. Of course, he'd already told her that he wanted her to feel free to ask him anything, but there were some things that were just harder than others, and that was one that would be difficult for her at any point, but especially now when they were just getting to know each other.

As the service ended, they stood, her children filing out behind them and Wilson casually putting an arm on her shoulder, she assumed to keep them together and not necessarily because he wanted to touch her.

There were some quizzical looks and a couple of raised brows, but no one asked, even though everyone had seen them sitting together, and she knew the rumors were going to be running rampant.

"We could have asked Pastor Connelly to announce that you and I are engaged and going to be married tomorrow. That would have saved us all of these looks." Wilson spoke quietly into her ear, low enough that she was the only one who could hear.

She turned and smiled at him. "Do they bother you?"

"Not at all. I was thinking more along the lines they were probably bothering you."

"They don't bother me a bit. They can wonder all they want. And if they ask, I can tell them that I am the most blessed person in the world."

"I'm sorry, but I think that's me."

They grinned at each other and then walked into the fellowship hall, where food was set out on tables.

"Excuse me while I elbow my way to your pie before it's gone," Wilson said. Then he grinned. "Can I get you anything?"

"I'll settle the kids at a table, and whatever you bring back, we'll be happy for."

"Can I go with him?" Gifford asked, and Charity's heart skipped a beat. Gifford had been a little standoffish with Wilson, and she hoped this meant he was warming up to him.

So this new development of Gifford wanting to go with Wilson encouraged Charity. But she didn't want Wilson to have to take him if he didn't want to.

"Sure. You can tell me what everyone likes. All I know is I want a piece of your mom's pie."

"Mom makes the best pie," Gifford said as they walked away.

Charity watched them go, her heart feeling warm and happy. When had that become a normal feeling for her? She wasn't sure, but the idea of being happy wasn't as foreign as it had seemed even a few weeks ago. Maybe she wasn't quite looking forward to the rest of her life, but it didn't seem so bleak and empty and hard and full of struggle. And it was all because of one man. One man who had decided to follow the Lord.

That thought made her lips turn down. Not because she wasn't happy that Wilson wanted to do what God wanted him to, but it was more because she remembered that Wilson wasn't with her because of her. She knew that shouldn't bother her, she should just be happy with what she'd been given, but she wanted him to...like her, be attracted to her, she supposed, although that was so far out she almost laughed aloud. She, a mother of five and definitely not in Wilson's league, was not the kind of person who Wilson would ever be attracted to.

"Hey, Charity."

Charity turned to see Amy, Wilson's sister who had just gotten married, standing behind her holding a cup of hot chocolate.

"Hey," she said, feeling a little tongue-tied. She wanted to make a good impression on Wilson's family, and while they were all very nice people, and she probably didn't need to worry, there was just something inside of her that didn't want them to pity her.

"Judd is going to be driving the horses on a short ride as soon as he gets them hitched up. I just wanted to make sure that you knew that your kids are invited," Amy said, smiling and looking friendly and happy with her rosy cheeks and her sparkling eyes. Marriage agreed with her.

"And I'll be there to supervise the situation, just in case you're concerned that there will be an adult in the group." Jones walked over, putting an arm around Amy and pulling her toward him. She leaned easily on his chest while still smiling at Charity.

Amy laughed and swatted him. "I'm an adult."

"Charity knows what I mean," Jones said with a wink.

"I'm sure my children would love to do that."

"We're not going to have as many as we usually do Sunday mornings, and if you'd like me to take Evans, I can keep an eye on him," Amy offered.

"Sure. I'm sure he will love it. Actually, speaking of, I haven't made it to the nursery yet, but I need to go pick them up."

"Serafina is welcome too. I didn't mean to exclude her. She's old enough and has gone before, so I figured you knew we were expecting you to send her."

"Of course. Thank you so much. They just love riding behind the horses."

Amy grinned and glanced at Jones who was looking down at her with such a sweet expression of love and admiration it made Charity's heart clench as they walked off together.

She hurried to the nursery, thanking the workers and getting both of her children, along with their diaper bag.

"I totally forgot about picking the kids up." Wilson's voice came in her ear as she lifted the baby bag onto her shoulder and turned, holding Evans in one arm and holding Serafina's hand in the other.

Without saying anything more, he took Evans out of her arms. It surprised Charity that Evans went willingly. Normally after he'd been in the nursery for a while, he was clingy until he had been assured that his mother wasn't going to leave him again anytime soon.

"It's not your job to pick them up," she said easily.

"There are two kids, and it's easier if you have help. That's my job. As the dad."

His words hung in the air between them. The hall was deserted and was just the two of them, so the words rang extra loud.

"I'm sorry. You're right. If you're going to be a dad, you do need to learn to do these things."

"To remember to do them. I have to remember before I can learn." He said that, and it felt like the awkwardness disappeared.

She didn't know why the idea of him being a dad felt so...weird. Because she knew that was his plan.

Still, it had taken her a little bit unaware, and she hugged those words to her heart. How could she have been so blessed? This man who wanted to marry her didn't just want to take care of her, protect her, and provide for her children, he wanted to be a dad. To give her children the male influence that they needed in their lives, to give her a helping hand, taking care of their children together. Their children. Not hers, theirs.

Was it really real? It seemed to be. He didn't seem to think anything of it as they walked out together, him chatting with Evans as they moved to where Gifford and Banks sat together at the far table, pie in front of them.

"I hope it was okay that I got the boys some pie. I didn't think to ask."

"And I didn't think to ask if it was okay if they went on the sleigh ride that Amy and Jones and Judd are offering as soon as they get the horses hitched up. I told Amy they'd be there. She even said she'd take Evans."

"That's fine. I guess we each have some adjustments to make." His eyes, sparkling but serious, glanced down at her.

She nodded. "The pie is fine. It's Christmas Eve. I hardly think it's going to hurt them. Plus, it's a special day."

"That's what I thought, but I should have asked. We'll figure it out."

"I suppose. I appreciate you not being upset with me."

"I could say the same thing. After all, I'm a newcomer, and you are already set in your ways, so I want this adjustment to not be too much."

"We both need to adjust. If you're helping, it should be both of us making decisions, not just me."

"I'm definitely helping. I guess we didn't really talk about that, but that was my plan."

"I'm kind of figuring that out, and I appreciate it. More than I can say, to be honest."

As they reached the table, she looked around, finding Lavinia playing with a few other girls across the fellowship hall.

"I'm going to run and get Lavinia, so she can eat too. That way, she'll be around when they're ready to go for the ride."

"Sounds good," he said. "I'll get everybody settled and wait on you."

"Thanks," she said. It was unusual for her to be able to leave her children to go get another. Normally she would have to drag both Evans and Serafina with her in order to get Lavinia, since she couldn't leave either one of them unattended at the table.

Having someone helping her was going to take a little bit of time to get used to. But that feeling of the future having promise, rather than just looking bleak, grew more pronounced.

It wasn't long till she had Lavinia back at the table, with the rest of the kids, where Wilson had put a piece of pie and got a drink for each of them except for the youngest two.

He even had a piece for her. She couldn't remember the last time someone had gotten her a piece of pie, or food of any kind, and brought it to her. Other than yesterday when he'd taken her out for lunch.

Maybe her life really was going to change. How could she not admire Wilson for instigating all of those changes?

She sat down, and he said a short prayer, and then like a real family, they started eating together.

The kids had barely finished their pie when Amy came to the door and announced that the kids were invited to go for a sleigh ride.

"Make sure you keep your coats on, guys," she said as Gifford and Banks got up to run to the door.

"If you give me Serafina, I'll take her and Evans, and I'll ride along," Wilson offered, holding his hand out for Serafina who had been sitting on Charity's lap.

Her brows rose. But she didn't say anything, just made sure Serafina's face was wiped, put her hat down on her head, and handed her over.

He gave her a jaunty smile and then walked out with Serafina in one arm, Evans in the other, and Lavinia walking beside him. The boys scooted on ahead, but occasionally they looked back to make sure that he was coming.

"He's quite a guy, isn't he?" Kyra said as she settled into the space that the children had left.

"I can't quite believe he's real. If that means he's quite a guy, then so be it."

"Yeah. I'm pretty sure that means he's quite a guy." Kyra looked after him, then smiled as she glanced back at Charity. "You look shell-shocked." She tilted her head. "Are you not happy?"

"I… I'm having trouble processing everything. But I'm definitely happy. I just can't believe that it's going to last, you know? I mean, it's one thing to deal with kids for a little bit, it's another thing to handle the drudgery of day in and day out." Plus, there was the little fact that he didn't really love her and wasn't marrying her because he wanted to spend more time with her. But that wasn't necessarily something she wanted to talk about.

"Why don't you just trust? Trust the Lord, trust Wilson, and let go. It's like you're almost afraid that if you think that things are going to be happy, they're going to evaporate in front of you."

"Well, that's been my experience."

"But you can't let that color the rest of your life, you know?" Kyra lifted a shoulder and glanced around the room. "I'm not really a good person to talk. You know I'm not married and I have no prospects. And here you are a mother of five, with far more experience than I have with men and motherhood."

"Just because I have experience doesn't make me wise," Charity said, knowing it was true.

"All right, I guess I just feel like you need to enjoy it. It might not last. You might be right. But if you keep yourself from enjoying it now, does it make it any different when it finally ends? Other than you were miserable the whole time, instead of being miserable with the ending."

"I guess I feel like I don't have as far to fall when everything gets pulled out from under me, if I'm not enjoying it. You know? Like, you have a much harder landing if you never saw the end coming and didn't prepare for it."

Kyra nodded and seemed to understand. "I can understand what you're saying. But you see my point?"

"I do. And you're right. I might as well enjoy it. It might not last. Maybe he'll figure out that this was a lot harder than what he thought it was going to be."

"And maybe he'll fall in love with you, and he'll dig in, and he'll be there for the long haul, and the two of you will grow old together, and yeah, it'll be hard, there will be heartbreak, there will be times where you cry, but that's the way life is. It is not just you having a husband who leaves you with five small children. Yeah, that was pretty big. But every life has big and little problems."

Kyra looked at her, sincere, like she wanted Charity to understand.

And Charity knew she was right. She knew that there were lots of problems in the world, she wasn't the only one. She wasn't even the only one whose husband had left, and there were worse things that could happen. Maybe not in a relationship, but she could have had cancer when he left, or he could have left her with a child in the hospital. But all of her children were healthy, she was healthy, and she should look at her blessings, rather than being scared to embrace them, for fear that they would disappear.

"I needed that talk today. Thank you," she said, smiling at her friend and truly appreciating the fact that Kyra had seen something off and hadn't been afraid to tell her about it.

"All right, you know you can go out and watch. They're going up and down the street, so your kids will enjoy waving to you as they go by if you're out there standing."

"All right. That's a good idea." Charity and Kyra stood and walked out, and just as Kyra had said, the horses and wagon were coming back down the street with the kids singing Christmas carols at the top of their lungs and only occasionally Amy's sweet soprano to be heard above the din.

Wilson seemed to be having a good time, with Serafina and Evans sitting on his lap. His back was toward Charity as they came down the street, but Gifford and Banks saw her and waved excitedly, calling out to her. That made Wilson turn, and he gave her a grin, pointing her out to Serafina and Evans who both managed to get chubby little hands in the air and move them back and forth.

She was not used to such a sweet sight, to see her kids having a good time, and to see a man who had been willing to step in and give her a hand. She determined in her heart that she would be the best wife that she could possibly be, although her confidence in her ability to be a good wife was probably at an all-time low. After all, Clancy had told her she was a terrible wife, and that was the reason he had to find someone else.

But maybe Kyra's advice could apply to that situation as well. After all, Clancy was in the wrong. No matter how bad of a wife she was, he never should have left her, and if she looked on the bright side, she had learned a few things, and she would be a better wife now than she ever had been before.

Chapter Fourteen

"I now pronounce you man and wife. Ladies, may I present to you Mr. and Mrs. Wilson McBride," the preacher intoned, serious and sober, even though they were standing in Charity's living room and the only witnesses they had were the pastor's wife and Wilson's mother.

Wilson and Charity had talked about inviting his family to witness their nuptials, but they hated to interrupt everyone on Christmas Day. If they weren't getting married, Wilson would be taking a nap right now. They'd already opened the gifts, eaten a large meal which Wilson had helped her prepare, and had spent some time at his mother's house. Where Charity's children had met all their new cousins. It was so odd, blending a family together.

"Congratulations, son." His mother came over, and he leaned down, giving her a hug and kissing her on the cheek. She looked extremely happy, and he hoped it was all happiness that caused her eyes to tear up. He hadn't meant to give her a moment of worry, although he supposed he should have known that she was going to be a little concerned when he announced he was marrying a woman that he barely knew and didn't love.

Charity was beautiful. There was no other way to describe her as he glanced over at her. That odd swirling happened in his chest again as she hugged his mother, and his mother put her arm around her and they walked away, chatting.

She was so humble, so willing to learn, so eagerly desiring to do her best at whatever was in front of her, whether it was being a wife and mother, or whether it was cooking a meal. He appreciated the fact that she cared and wanted to be a blessing to people. Even though she could barely keep her head up herself.

He walked over to Pastor Connelly who was tucking his books away.

"I really appreciate you coming out on Christmas," he said, handing the pastor several folded hundred-dollar bills. It was more than double what the pastor said he usually charged for weddings, just because it was on Christmas.

"Thank you," Pastor Connelly said, taking the money and sliding it in his shirt pocket. "It's my pleasure. I have a good feeling about the direction that the two of you are headed. I like seeing the families knitted together, rather than torn apart. And to see one stitched back together after being brutally ripped to pieces makes my heart happy."

There was a bit of sadness still in his tone, and Wilson could only guess that it was probably because the family wouldn't have needed to be stitched back together if the man that Charity had married hadn't abdicated his responsibilities and run off. But that man's loss was Wilson's gain. He'd almost come full circle and believed that God, rather than thinking that Wilson would be good for Charity, had known all along that Wilson needed Charity and her children. He could already see the changes that had occurred in his thinking and in his life. How he'd grown closer to the Lord. How he'd seen the strength and resilience with which Charity lived her life and even... He felt that part of him that had always longed to be paired up with someone to walk through life with reaching out and feeling like Charity was exactly the right person to spend the rest of his life with.

"It makes my heart happy too. I think I've known I needed Charity and the children, and I think it just took me a little bit of time to realize that it wasn't for Charity's benefit, but for my own."

"That's a mature way of looking at it," Pastor Connelly said as he slowly walked beside Wilson to the door.

"You're welcome to stay, there's plenty of leftovers from lunch, and Charity has a pie that she hasn't cut but has been saving for this occasion."

"I think the Mrs. and I would like to get home and take a nap," Pastor Connelly said with a smile as he looked over at his wife who was obviously saying goodbye to the ladies.

"I understand that desire. I think with children though, my naptime is going to be limited."

"For a while. But then, the kids grow up and you get that time back again. It just seems like it'll never end while you're in it, but one day it does, and then you miss it."

"That's what I hear," Wilson said, knowing that his mother had said something very similar to him.

"So, son, I've been thinking about this whole marriage of convenience thing," Pastor Connelly said, looking around and lowering his voice.

Wilson lowered his head so that he could hear a little better. "And?"

"And I think that men and women are a little different. I know you know that, but I just wanted to remind you and to let you know that I think it might be a good idea for you to...to know each other a while before you...move on, if you know what I mean."

He assumed the pastor was talking about intimacy, although he didn't come right out and say it. But nothing else seemed to fit.

Wilson nodded. "I wondered how long."

He felt like he was ready tonight. He had a certain little feeling every time he looked at Charity. She wasn't hard to look at, and for Wilson, marriage always meant that it came with certain benefits. That wasn't the reason he wanted to get married soon, but he certainly wasn't going to turn that down since it came with the territory.

He had agreed to sleep on the couch tonight, but he assumed that when they moved to his house, they would be sharing a room and a bed together.

"Well, I couldn't tell you for sure how long, but it seems to me that if you were dating or courting, you would spend six months or a year getting to know each other. That seems applicable here. I would say a year, just to be on the safe side."

A year? Wilson tried not to look too dismayed. He had been thinking a couple of weeks, not...a year?

But he respected the pastor's opinion and knew that the man wanted the very best for them and their marriage.

"You want to build a strong foundation. A good, solid friendship. You want to trust each other. You don't want the physical side to get in the way of building something that will last a lifetime. Remember, son, you're probably more eager for the marriage bed than she is, and if you give her time to adjust, to get used to you, and don't push her, you'll have something better than if you rush in."

"I understand." He didn't like it, wasn't very happy about that, but he understood. It would take Charity a little longer to get used to him. That made sense.

"Are you sure a year?" he asked, just to confirm. Maybe the pastor actually meant a month and got a little confused about what he was saying.

"I believe that to be a good idea. There are no stipulations in the Bible, so I can't give you a chapter and verse. But I do know that if you were getting to know each other without being married first, you would spend approximately a year doing that. Some people get married in a shorter amount of time, some people spend longer."

Wilson wanted to ask about the verse where Paul said it was better to marry than to burn, but he figured Pastor Connelly knew that verse and was giving his advice with that in mind.

Of course, Wilson was already married. Although he didn't feel that way. And he still hadn't remembered to get rings. Well, the jewelry store had probably been open yesterday, but he hadn't had time to go check.

Still, would a ring make him feel more married? He didn't figure it would.

"All right. I can see God's hand of blessing on this marriage, and I wish you the very best," Pastor Connelly said as his wife came over and he put his arm around her, and they walked out the door together.

Somehow seeing them leave made Wilson feel bereft. Which was so odd. Maybe it was the idea that he had a whole year in front of him and he needed to look at it in a different way. It wasn't about denying himself, it was about courting Charity. He needed to spend that year courting his wife, wooing her, doing all the things that he didn't do before they were married, so that next year this time, she was comfortable with him and looked at him like someone she wouldn't mind sharing a bed with and waking up beside.

He nodded his head. He could do it. He could get advice from someone. Someone who knew what women wanted and could guide him in that direction. After all, the Bible said that he was supposed to dwell with his wife according to knowledge. He should know her, should know everything he could about her, and he had a whole year to do that. And then, after that, he had the rest of his life for the things that he was most eager for. He could wait.

Chapter Fifteen

"And even though the wise men didn't actually come on Christmas, since we're celebrating the birth of Jesus, we kind of lump it all in together, and that's how we end up with wise men at the manger scene on Christmas," Wilson said, sitting on the floor beside the bunk beds where Gifford and Banks were already tucked in.

Charity stood at the door, smiling at the scene. The only light in the room was a nightlight, and she could see the outline of Wilson as he sat, looking toward the bed, his hands folded in his lap, his posture relaxed.

She had put Lavinia and the two little ones to bed, and Wilson was still chatting with the boys.

There was no doubt that he loved them.

"Good night, boys. Merry Christmas," she said, smiling as they repeated her words.

"I guess that means it's time for me to go. I'll see you fellas in the morning."

"Are you staying here tonight?" Gifford asked, sounding surprised.

"Sure am. I'll be staying with you guys from now on. That's what it meant when I married your mother."

"Until you leave," Banks said, sounding a little bit sad but mostly matter-of-fact like he knew what was going to happen, and he didn't need Wilson to tell him.

"I'm not leaving. Not till God takes me."

Charity knew that meant death, but she wasn't quite sure the kids knew that.

"Like God took our dad?" Gifford asked.

"No. Your father left because he wanted to. What Wilson is saying is that he's not leaving until God takes him to heaven. Otherwise, he's going to be here, with us."

Charity hoped he didn't mind that she stepped in, but she had been afraid that was what the boys were going to assume. And they couldn't be more wrong. She wanted to make sure that they weren't applying what had happened to them with their dad to Wilson. And thinking that Wilson was the same kind of man, since he was not.

Water dripped in the bathroom, the leaky faucet Clancy had always said he was going to fix and never had, and it didn't matter to Charity anyway. Whether he fixed it, whether he didn't, it was just the idea that there were a lot of things he said he was going to do and ended up not doing. It was just one more broken promise in a whole string of them.

"Your mother's right. That's exactly what I meant."

There was silence from the boys, and then Wilson said, "Good night. Merry Christmas, boys."

"Merry Christmas," the boys repeated together.

Charity slipped back out of the room, and Wilson walked out behind her, softly closing the door.

"The other ones are in bed?" Wilson asked.

She nodded.

"All right then. I guess our work is done. I'm going to head back downstairs. I'll see you in the morning."

She opened her mouth. She had thought that maybe they were going to...sit together, cuddle...kiss?

She knew it was kind of soon for that. He didn't really know her, and maybe he would never want to kiss her. Maybe he would never be attracted to her. Not the way she was to him.

She bit back the disappointment, trying to remember what Kyra had said about being thankful for what she had and appreciating it. Maybe that wasn't exactly what Kyra had said, but that was what she had turned it into. She had to be grateful for what she had been given and not wish for more, like a husband who thought she was the most beautiful woman in the world and admired and was attracted to her.

"All right," she said, trying not to sound disappointed at all. In fact, she actually sounded cheerful, and she was kind of proud about that. "Merry Christmas. Thank you so much for making our Christmas extra super special."

"I think you did the same to mine."

He was just saying that, but it was nice of him, and she nodded her head as he turned and walked down the stairs.

She wasn't used to not walking around checking the doors, closing up, making sure everything was turned off before she headed upstairs for the last time. But Wilson would take care of it. And he would be down there if anything happened in the middle of the night. He would be there to help her. The idea was vastly reassuring and reminded her that she had one more thing to be thankful for. She was no longer the sole adult in the house, responsible for all five children on her own. She often wondered if something happened how she was going to save all five of her kids. She finally had to give it over to the Lord because the idea scared her, because she knew she couldn't do it.

But now she didn't have to worry. Because of Wilson.

She walked slowly to her room, giving thanks for the Secret Saint who had provided all the gifts for her children. Their Christmas had been happy and joyful, rather than sad and disappointing. Not that material things should matter, but it was fun to give gifts and fun to receive them. And that was part of the reason they gave gifts on Christmas, because God had given them the gift of his son.

She'd never quite thought about it in that respect before, but she wondered if God enjoyed giving gifts as much as she did. If God enjoyed seeing them appreciate His gifts as much as she enjoyed seeing her children's happy faces as they opened their presents.

Probably. Actually, she was sure that He did. He loved seeing her appreciation for what He had done for her, and it made her even more determined to make sure that she showed her gratefulness and spoke her thanks as often as she could to the Lord. After all, He had been so very, very good to her.

Chapter Sixteen

"You seem extra thoughtful tonight," Terry said as she came over to Judd's chair and began to knead his shoulders gently.

He closed his eyes. Terry had been the best thing that had ever happened to him. He wasn't quite sure why God saw fit to give him such an amazing wife, but he was very, very grateful.

Her fingers worked magic on his shoulders, and he felt his whole body relaxing.

"I guess it's a thoughtful night." It was Christmas night. They had spent most of the day at Terry's family's house. There was so much going on with her siblings, with all the kids, and the excitement and the happiness of watching them open their gifts, and seeing the family banter and enjoy each other's company. It couldn't compare to going to his house where his mother required formal dress and the dinner conversation was boring, at best.

But they were finally home, and he had settled himself in the recliner after building a fire for them both to enjoy.

"Is that all it is?" Terry asked gently, and he knew that was her way of saying that if he didn't want to tell her, he didn't have to. But he always wanted to tell her everything. There were just some things he couldn't.

But since things had worked out for Wilson, he supposed it was okay for him to say this one thing.

"I've lost my partner in the Secret Saint endeavors."

"You have?" she asked, her voice surprised, her fingers stilling for a moment before they started again, soothing and relaxing his muscles.

"I did. I'm a little bummed about it."

"Who?" she asked, and then she added immediately, "If you can tell me."

"I think I can. Since he has officially quit his duties." Terry wrote for the town social media site, and her specific job was to detail the actions of the Secret Saint and postulate on his identity. That was part of the reason that Judd had not shared this information with her previously.

"Who?" she asked, her fingers remaining gentle despite the excitement in her voice.

"Your brother, Wilson."

Her fingers stopped completely, and she moved around his chair to stand in front of him, her hands on her hips.

"No way. You're kidding, right?" She tilted her head and looked at him as though she were trying to tell whether he was lying or not. He knew she knew that he was honest, so he wasn't worried about that, but it probably was taking her a little bit of extra time to adjust to this.

"It's true. Wilson was my partner and most of the time the one who came up with the ideas. And who was in a better position to do it than Wilson? After all, he's got your mom's contacts with all of her friends, plus all of your siblings. He pretty much is connected to everything in the town of Mistletoe Meadows."

"That makes perfect sense. Half the time, I wondered if my mom was involved."

"She doesn't know. At least as far as I know, she doesn't know."

"Not unless Wilson would have told her. But I don't think he had. I don't think he's told anyone, or surely I would have heard about it."

"He will play this pretty tight to the vest, and now that you're in the position that you're in, no one's probably going to be telling you anything."

"I know. It stinks. Except, I'm actually in on it." She grinned and knelt down in front of him, picking up one of his stocking feet and rubbing the bottom of it.

His eyes drifted until they were half closed, and he grinned at her. "I knew there was a reason I married you."

"Oh, stop. You've done so much for me, and I feel bad that I'm not around as much as I would like to be. The practice has kept me busier than I thought."

"That's because people love you. And people from other towns are coming here. You know you could close and stop accepting new patients."

"I know. I should do that or hire another doctor to work with me." She sighed. "I spent all my life so far studying and working, and I know that this is my time to earn money, and I started later than most people did, but... I just want to be with you. I know that's normal for newlyweds, but it's a real effort to get out of bed and go to work in the morning."

"We didn't have to do it today."

"And I don't have to do it tomorrow either. What do you suppose we ought to do?"

"I don't know. You tell me," he said, his eyes glinting at her.

They grinned together, and he had a pretty good idea of what they would be doing tomorrow morning, and he was definitely looking forward to it.

"What about children?" Terry asked after she rubbed his foot for a little longer.

He didn't say anything right away, and she carefully put that foot down and picked up his other foot, ministering to it the same way, and he found himself working hard to not fall asleep.

Children. What did he think about them?

"Well, we had a wagon full of children this evening, and I thought that was fun. Mostly because all I had to do was drive the horses."

"You were an only child. Maybe you don't like kids?"

"What does being an only child have to do with liking children?"

"I'm sorry. I suppose you're right. That wasn't fair."

"No, I understood what you were saying. My parents obviously had a different philosophy than yours, and you are wondering if I share it."

"Something we probably should have talked about before we got married."

"Why? If you don't want any kids, I'm okay with that, and if you want twenty, I'm okay with that too. As long as I get you in the bargain."

"Really? You don't care?"

She sounded so shocked, he felt like he needed to go back over in his mind what he truly believed. "I guess I really enjoy being at your family's with all the hubbub and the craziness and all that, but I know that for you, you've worked hard to be where you are, and if you have children, you're probably going to need someone else to watch them for you. I can help in the off-season, and if you want me to, I could even quit my job and raise them for us, but I guess you're the one who is going to be the most impacted."

"If you quit your job, it will impact you."

"Not like it would impact you. I haven't worked for the last twelve years to get a degree so that I can practice."

"True. Still, this isn't just about me. It has to be about us. Otherwise, it's not fair."

"A lot of times, the things in life aren't fair."

"I know that's true."

She set his foot down gently and moved closer to him, running both hands up and down his calves. That felt almost as good as what she had done to his feet.

"I want you to have an opinion. It bothers me that you don't."

"What's your opinion?" he asked, feeling bad that he had disappointed her. He didn't want to, but what he had said was true. Whatever worked for her would work for him. He would make sure of it.

"I want a family like I grew up in. I love having a lot of siblings, but I also want to work. You're right. I spent more than eight years in school to be able to do what I'm doing now. I don't want to not do it. It's important to me."

"So there you go. That's why my opinion has to be fluid, because you're the one who's caught in the dilemma."

"Maybe once I get my student loans paid off, and I can quit my job if I want to, we can have as many kids as God gives us?"

"If you want to wait that long."

She paused, looking up at him like she was trying to figure out what he was trying to say. He waited.

"You think I might...be too old by the time I have everything paid off and I'm financially ready to have children?"

"Maybe?" He didn't know. There were advances in medical techniques which he knew she would know more about than he did, but nothing was guaranteed. "Even if you were young, there's no guarantee that you could have children. You know? It's kind of arrogant to assume that as soon as we're ready, God will be ready to bless us."

"It is." She sat thoughtfully, and he waited. He supposed if he thought about it, he'd really want children, and especially now that he had Terry. Because he wouldn't want to have them with just anyone.

"And there's no guarantee that I'll be any kind of a good dad. I guess I worry about that a little bit too. Since you're right, I was an only child, and I didn't really see my parents parent anything other than me, and I wasn't exactly a difficult child."

"My mom is full of wisdom." She paused, and then she said, "But she's getting older every year too. There is no guarantee that she'll be around if we wait to have kids."

"Maybe it's not supposed to be our decision." He just let that statement hang as she thought about it.

"You mean, we should allow God to decide?"

"Isn't it funny that we say 'allow' like we're in charge. When in reality, He made the universe, He made us, how dare we think we know better than Him?"

"All right. That was a pretty powerful statement, and I think you're right on every level. I can't decide anyway. So why don't I just take it out of my hands, because maybe it shouldn't have been there to begin with."

"Maybe," he said as she straightened, putting her arms on his legs and leaning toward him.

"Now. It's Christmas, and we're done with all the festivities, and we're home at last. What do you think we ought to do?"

He grinned, because she really didn't need to ask him. There was only one thing he wanted to do. Be with her.

"Come here," he said, lifting her gently and setting her in his lap. "This is a better place to think about something as difficult as that. I'm sure if we spend enough time thinking about it, we can figure something out."

Her lips touched his temple while his fingers ran up her arm. "You think?"

"Yeah. We're reasonably intelligent, and together we're sure to come up with something."

She smiled as her lips trailed down his cheek, and finally they met his, and maybe they were both reasonably intelligent, but he didn't do much thinking after that.

Chapter Seventeen

"**D**o you think he's asleep?"

The words came to Wilson from what felt like very far away.

"I don't know. His eyes are closed. He's making those loud noises that Dad used to make."

"Snoring. He's snoring."

That was Gifford. He recognized his voice, so the other voices must've been maybe Banks and Lavinia?

But that was weird, because what were they doing in his house? Oh. They were going to move there. But wait, it was the day after Christmas. Wasn't Christmas just yesterday? That meant today was the day after Christmas, and he...

Wilson opened his eyes, looking up at three sets of eyes staring back down at him.

"He's awake!" Lavinia said, jumping up and down. "Would you play with us?" she asked, pausing to step closer and lean back over top of him.

"I don't think he knows where he is," Gifford said, squinting, and that's when Wilson fully awoke.

He was on the couch, where he lay down after he had checked the doors and windows and made sure everything was turned off last night, wishing that he could have had Charity beside him for a little while, sitting on the couch, looking at the tree they put up and decorated, seeing the gifts that were scattered around, and enjoying a peaceful Christmas night together. Their first night as a married couple.

But the pastor had said he needed to give her a year, and if he sat snuggled up next to her on the couch every night, it wasn't going to be a year.

One day down, 364 more days to go. It felt like forever.

But he couldn't fault the pastor for his reasoning. And he wanted to build a relationship that lasted for a lifetime. Not only did Charity not deserve to have another man who didn't stay, but she deserved to have the very best relationship a couple could have, and he was determined to give it to her. And if that meant that he would be sleeping on the couch for the next year and not snuggling there in the evening with his wife, then so be it.

"Are you awake?" Banks said, and Wilson focused his eyes on the little boy.

"I am. I guess I'm just not used to having a welcoming committee whenever I come back to consciousness in the morning."

"What?" Lavinia said, scrunching up her nose and looking so much like her mother that it gave Wilson's heart a pang.

"I need you guys to move back so I can sit up," Wilson said, instead of repeating what he'd already said, when she wasn't going to understand anyway.

He supposed this was his new reality. Children staring at him from the time he woke up in the morning until the time he went to bed at night, and always wanting to do something with him. Which, honestly, he didn't mind at all. It reminded him of his childhood. He'd always wanted to spend more time with his dad and hadn't had a chance, and now it was his turn to be the dad. He was looking forward to it. Except, he did want to have some time alone with his wife. Although, maybe that was not a wise thing either. Not if he was going to spend the next year courting her. They probably should be chaperoned by the children, and that would ensure that his behavior stayed within bounds.

Built-in chaperones. Nice.

"You guys want some breakfast?" he asked as he sat up and considered standing. He was a little bit sore, not being used to sleeping on the couch, and it sagged a good bit in the middle, but it was just until they got moved into his house.

"Yay! Let's have pancakes!" Lavinia said sweetly, slipping her hand into his as he stood to his feet.

"All right. Pancakes it is. As long as I can find the ingredients," he amended as he slipped out from behind the coffee table. "You guys are going to have to let me use the restroom first, and then we'll see if we've got the ingredients for pancakes, okay?"

"All right! I'll tell Mom you're up," Banks said, running to the bottom of the stairs before Wilson could stop him.

"Hold up. If your mom isn't up, why don't we let her sleep in a little bit today. She's probably extra tired because Christmas is extra busy for moms."

"Okay. But we'll give her pancakes, won't we?"

"We'll make special pancakes just for her, if she's down before we're done." Wilson had a feeling that all the noise downstairs would definitely be waking her up, but maybe she really was tired and wouldn't be up for a while.

He hardly imagined that a mom would have the luxury of sleeping in much, and he wished he could give that to her. But he wasn't sure he could go up and get Serafina and Evans up by himself.

Although Gifford could probably help him. But he promised pancakes, so he probably ought to do that.

The kids were waiting for him when he made his way to the kitchen.

"Pancakes are everybody's favorite," Lavinia said as he opened up the cupboard doors, looking for flour.

He was a little bit aghast at how bare the cupboards were. How was she feeding five children three times a day with cupboards that were mostly full of air?

They'd had a big Christmas meal the day before, but the Secret Saint had made sure that they were stocked up on all things necessary to provide that meal. He had been behind all that.

Would Charity be upset about that if she found out?

He hardly thought she would, but there was also no reason for her to find out, either.

"Can I help? Mom always lets me help!" Banks said as he finally found the flour, sugar, and salt and set them down on the table.

"I was hoping you would," he said, smiling at Banks. Gifford stood back, watching.

"I thought you were going to help too," Wilson said, nodding at Gifford.

"Mom lets me pour the batter on the hot griddle sometimes."

"All right. That'll be your job. Can you get the griddle out?" He looked around, unable to even see where the griddle might be.

"Mom keeps it over here, because there's not much room in the kitchen. She says our kitchen is the size of a postage stamp." Gifford spoke as he walked over to the couch and pulled the griddle out from underneath it.

He'd never seen anyone store their griddle under the couch before, but...he supposed when a person had five children, they had to get creative when they lived in a small house.

He shook his head, smiling.

"Don't you need a recipe?" Banks asked as he started to measure flour in a bowl.

"I have it in my head," he said, grinning at their wide eyes.

"Mom always uses a recipe."

"That's probably because she has so much information about all of her children in her head that she doesn't have room for recipes," Wilson postulated. "Or maybe, she just hasn't made pancakes as much as I have."

"They're only for special occasions, because Mom says it takes too long to get five kids ready in the morning, and so she makes things that don't take as much time."

"I see. Well, all I have to do this morning is make pancakes, so I guess it's a special occasion."

"Is it a special occasion when the dad is in the kitchen?" Charity said, and the sound of her voice made him turn and get warm all over.

She had Evans on one hip, and Serafina held her hand as they stood there. But he didn't notice the children as much as he noticed the rosy cheeks of his wife, the smiling eyes, and the way her hair waved around her face. Maybe there was a little bit of sadness on her face, and he wondered at that. Was there something wrong? Was she regretting the fact that they had gotten married yesterday?

He hated that he hadn't been with her last night, didn't know what she was thinking, couldn't talk to her as the doubts rolled in and help her keep them away. He had a few doubts of his own, although mostly they were related to whether or not he could be a good husband and a good father, stepping into someone else's role and taking on five children at once. It felt like a huge undertaking and one he wasn't sure he was ready for.

He wouldn't have minded having her snuggled up against him, telling him that everything was going to be okay. That they would trust in the Lord and do the best they could. Wasn't that what being married was? Having someone beside you to stand shoulder to shoulder with you while you faced the world. To remind you of what the Bible said when you forgot, just as you reminded them.

"I think it's a special occasion when Mom is in the kitchen with Dad," he said and was rewarded with a smile that reached her eyes and drove the sadness away. "The kids just said that it had to be a special occasion when we made pancakes. So, I think we have to make something up, since it isn't anyone's birthday, and yesterday was Christmas."

"Well, since yesterday was Christmas, we can celebrate our

wedding today," she said, lifting her brow and looking around at the children who clapped and cheered, like she'd suggested they all eat cake for breakfast and watch cartoons all day.

Wilson laughed. Sometimes children were just the easiest thing ever, and then sometimes it didn't matter what a person did, he couldn't make them happy.

He heard that about women too, but Charity didn't seem to be like normal women. She seemed to be happy no matter what or at least able to talk herself out of being upset.

Maybe someday he'd be able to tell her how much he appreciated that about her.

"Mr. Wilson said that I could run the griddle," Gifford announced to his mom as soon as the other kids were quiet enough for him to talk.

"Oh, he did?" she said, tilting her head and lifting her brows.

Gifford nodded, big nods where his chin bumped his chest with every downward turn of his head.

"Is that okay with you?" Wilson asked, although it was probably too late.

"If you think you can handle it."

"Oh, I know we can." He figured he'd be right there, able to supervise in case anything went wrong.

"All right then."

"And we don't need a recipe. He said the recipe is in his head."

"Impressive. So he's made pancakes a lot."

"When I was a kid," Wilson said as he got the measuring cup out and measured flour into a bowl, allowing Lavinia to dump it in, "I was responsible for breakfast one day every week. It runs in my mind it was usually Tuesdays. Pancakes was the meal that I always made. So yeah, I've made them for years, and I have the recipe memorized, although... I'm doubling it today."

"I hope there would have been as many people eating at your house."

"Terry was out of the house for years, and sometimes Isadora didn't eat much. And then she complained the pancakes were just big globs of carbs, and she ate fruit or something instead."

"Wow. I guess I kind of love big globs of carbs. I think I'll take a double portion."

Wilson laughed as he continued to allow Banks and Lavinia to help him measure the ingredients out and crack the eggs.

"Now, we're going to stir it all up, but we can't stir too much, because that's the key to good pancakes. Just stir until it's mixed, and no more."

"Really? That's the key?" Banks said, like he was remembering everything that Wilson told him for a future date.

It struck Wilson anew the responsibility he had to raise these children. They were looking at him, watching him, emulating him, and thinking about the things that he said and did. It felt like a heavy responsibility. And of course it was, but it was a responsibility that every man who had a child had.

Gifford put the first pancakes on the griddle, and Charity set the table with Serafina and Evans, and while they were waiting, he walked over to where Charity stood, washing off the utensils that they'd used and putting them in the drainboard.

He wanted to put his arm around her and nuzzle her cheek, maybe kiss her neck and tell her good morning, but Pastor Connelly had said he needed to wait a year, and that seemed a little forward for a couple who was supposed to be courting, even though they were married. So, he leaned his hip against the counter and shoved a hand in his pocket, feeling a little awkward, because he couldn't do what he wanted to do.

"Did you sleep well?"

He wanted to ask her a million other questions, like, did you change your mind? Are you still okay? Did you decide that you'd made a huge mistake and you want out of it? But he didn't.

"I did, surprisingly. I didn't realize how nervous I had been about being here by myself with all the children and if there was a bump in the night, it was all my responsibility. I just thought to myself,

'Wilson's down there now, and he'll take care of it,' and I laid my head down on the pillow and slept like a baby."

"I'm happy to hear that," he said.

"What about you? I always thought that couch was really comfortable. It sags through the middle, and I just love it."

He laughed. "That sag in the middle kind of made my hips hurt, but I walked it off. And I slept really well. So well in fact that the three oldest children were standing around me, staring down at me talking about me before I really even realized what was going on. I never heard them come downstairs."

"Oh, I'm so sorry. I'll say something to them—"

"No. It was fine. You wouldn't say something to them if I was their real dad. Would you?" He hated to use that word, "real." But it was true. If they were married and they were his kids and hers, she wasn't going to stop them from doing that if he allowed it.

"No. But... I don't mean to say they're not, it's just, I'm not sure that you'll tell them no if you don't want them to do something."

"Will it make you feel better if I promise you that I will tell them no if I don't want them to do something? Or maybe I should say if I feel like they're doing something they shouldn't do. Because it might not have been the best way to get woken up this morning, but when you're a dad, sometimes that's the way you get woken up and it has to be okay."

"You could have yelled at them and told them to leave you alone, that you were still sleeping."

"And then I would miss this time making pancakes with them. I'm glad I didn't. And I don't want to. I don't want to take the easy way out. I want to do the hard things. The hard things that dads do, when they're good dads. And they don't put themselves and their own comfort above their children."

"Wow. That's inspiring."

He chuckled, but he knew she was also serious. He didn't mean to be inspiring. He meant to be honest.

"So are you okay?" he asked, wanting to know if she changed her mind but not wanting to say it.

"Yes. I'm fine. How about you? I worry a little that after all the hubbub of yesterday, you would...regret what you'd done."

"Never."

She looked like she wanted to say a little bit more. And he thought for an instant that maybe they should talk about what the pastor had told him, but that kind of defeated the purpose, didn't it? He was supposed to be wooing her, courting her, not getting her input in everything, and if he did that, she might feel compelled to have to say that she didn't want to wait a year, because there might not be any way he could keep himself from saying that he didn't. And he didn't want to pressure her. The pastor was right, they needed to build a strong foundation, and that would be slowly and surely, over time.

"I didn't really have any plans for today, other than maybe starting to pack some things up."

"That sounds good to me. I was going to get some of my brothers together, and my brothers-in-law, and figured they could give us a hand between now and the new year, when they're not working as much. I actually think Jones has closed his clinic for the entire week. So he will probably be available almost any time."

"All right."

"I know you want the kids to take their naps in the afternoon, so not today, but maybe I can get some things in line for tomorrow, and maybe during that time, we can figure out exactly when we want to move everything so that we don't have one kid's bed here and another kid's bed there and we're trying to figure out how to put everybody to sleep some night."

"That makes a lot of sense. I suppose I should have been the one to think about that."

"I think you had enough to think about." He paused and then figured he'd better check. "It's still okay to move to my house?"

"Yes. And the sooner we can do that, the sooner we can get this up for sale."

"Sounds good to me."

"And I'll see if I can get in touch with Clancy and see how we're going to split the money for this. I hate to do it. But I might as well take the bull by the horns. Of course, I might not be able to get a hold of him. It's not like he left me contact info. All I have is his old phone number, which, unless he changed it, should still work."

"If not, we'll figure it out by going to a lawyer and seeing what they say. It will be nice to know, but I think probably we should just work on the assumption that you get half and he gets half, and if something else works out, we'll just be pleasantly surprised."

"That's a good idea."

"I think the pancakes are done. Would you come check them, Mr. Wilson?"

"We'll have to figure out what the kids are going to call you," Charity said softly as he started to move away.

His lips turned up in a smile as their eyes met. "Let's give them some time."

She nodded and looked happy that he suggested it, and he was glad he didn't insist. He would really like for them to call him Dad, it seemed a lot more casual than Mr. Wilson, but at the same time, they had a dad, and he hadn't been gone long. And Wilson didn't want to push in where he wasn't welcome or make the kids resent him. Maybe, the kids were an awful lot like Charity. They could just use a little bit of time.

Chapter Eighteen

"I'd like for you to go and get groceries this afternoon while the kids are sleeping," Wilson said to Charity three days later after they spent the morning moving things from her house to his.

The next day, they were moving all of the kids' beds and they would start staying at his place, even though there were still a few odds and ends to move out.

There were things that weren't going to fit in his house, and she would either have to put them in storage or, more likely, sell them. Or just let them go with the house.

She hadn't decided which. She didn't want to pay for storage, couldn't afford it, and while she wasn't attached to very many things, there was an end table that had been her grandmother's that she would like to keep.

"Okay," she said, focusing on what he had just told her. He'd like groceries.

She didn't have much money and had been waiting until someone had paid her for the holiday pies that she had made before she went. Honestly, she hadn't even considered that it would be more expensive to be eating with a man in the house. He liked to have meat with every meal, and she was used to getting by with cheap, inexpensive foods or mostly carbs and vegetables.

She tried to hide the growing panic in her chest, the way she felt when she was going to throw up, and didn't even notice that he had his wallet out until he waved it in front of her face.

"Take this. You can use any of the cards that are in there, and there is also cash. I'll text you the pin, I know this is terrible, but it's the same for every card."

He had multiple cards? And cash? Enough to buy groceries? Did he know how expensive groceries were?

He was used to only buying groceries for one person, though that one person ate more than her five kids put together.

She tried to shut that voice off in her head and just focus on taking things one thing at a time. There was no point getting upset and worried about it.

She took the wallet from him, her fingers brushing his, and she tried not to jerk back.

He didn't want her touching him, and he didn't have the same reaction she did, and she needed to be okay with that as well.

It all felt overwhelming, but she forced herself to give an easy smile and say, "Thank you. Is there anything in particular you would like?" There, she sounded completely normal, even kind and friendly.

"I eat whatever. I'm not picky. You get what you are comfortable making for the kids, and you know I'll eat along with you." He grinned, and she returned his smile. But his words didn't help her. She wanted to make things that he liked. She wanted to get the groceries that he wanted. Of course she knew what she would make for the kids, but she wanted to be considerate. It was kind of hard to do that though when the man wouldn't give her a hint of what that would be.

"You go on. I can put the kids down for their nap."

"All right. I'll text you when I'm leaving the store, and that way, you'll be around to help carry the stuff in."

"Sounds good," he said, but he didn't turn away. "I kind of wish I could go with you," he said. Then he shook his head. "That's weird, because I've always hated grocery shopping."

"I don't particularly like it either. I mean, I could spend all day in a candle shop, or clothing store, even a department store, but groceries? No, thank you."

"Well, I guess there are shops I could spend all day in, but they wouldn't have candles or clothes, except for maybe coveralls and work boots."

She laughed. She wouldn't mind going to that kind of store with him, just to see him interact with the things that he liked.

That was crazy. She was acting like a silly schoolgirl, who couldn't get enough of her current crush.

Except, she was much older than a schoolgirl, and she didn't have time for crushes. Not even if the object of her crush was her husband.

She walked out the door, feeling strangely tingly. Somehow, every interaction with him gave her a silly smile and made her heart feel warm and happy.

She wished it were the same for him and wondered for the millionth time if there was anything that she could do to get the man to fall in love with her, but she knew there really wasn't. People either felt that way about someone or they didn't. And those feelings were fleeting, she knew that, but...she wanted him to look at her like she was the only woman in the world.

She had gotten into her car before she came up with a brilliant idea if she did say so herself. Dialing Wilson's mother's number, she held her breath until the woman answered.

"Hello?"

"Hello, Marjorie. I am about to go grocery shopping for the first time since I married your son, and he told me to get whatever, because he's not picky. I was wondering if you could give me a little bit of guidance on what he likes, because even though I know he's not lying, he'll eat whatever I cook, I'd like to make things that he enjoys."

"Well, I can help you out with that. In fact, why don't you come on over, and I'll give you the recipes for some of his favorite meals."

She paused, then said, "Do you have time?"

"I sure do. I have time for any of my daughters, anytime they need me or I can give them a hand. Come on over."

"I'll be right there," she said, hanging up and starting her car, her chest feeling a hundred times lighter. Marjorie was the best.

And she did not disappoint. She met Charity at the door and guided her into her kitchen.

"Here's my recipe book, and if you want, to make it easy, you can just take pictures of his favorite meals, which I have marked with these Post-it notes. And you can go ahead and write them out later at your convenience or just keep them on your phone."

"Wow. That will be really handy. I'm so glad you thought of it."

"Well, I'm so glad you called. It's so much fun to be needed, and I do happen to know what he really likes. All of my kids can cook, and he had meals that he asked to learn how to make, because he liked them so much."

"Nice, so he can make these if he needs to."

"Oh, he can cook anything. He's a better cook than I am. Wilson… You probably already know this, but pretty much everything he touches turns to gold. We did call him the golden boy, because it seemed that way, but honestly, he's just the kind of person who really wants to do right. And I think that's why things always went well for him. He just seems to have God's favor."

"I don't know. I guess whatever he does, he does it well. And there doesn't seem to be anything he can't do, from changing a diaper, to making pancakes for the kids in the morning, to running a farm, to starting a successful business. I…sometimes feel a little outclassed." She stopped for a minute. "A lot outclassed, actually."

Marjorie's matronly eyes seemed to see right into her soul, but there was no doubt that the woman understood what she was saying.

"I think a lot of people who've been around Wilson feel like that. He's definitely one of a kind and just one of those people that other people have a hard time not liking, even if they're jealous of him."

"My kids even seem to like him, effortlessly. I'm not jealous that they sometimes prefer him over me, but... I'm surprised."

"That's Wilson. You're a lucky woman. But Wilson's more blessed than what he knows, I think."

Charity shook her head. "That's just the thing. I don't have anything to offer him."

"You're here, aren't you? You're humble enough to ask for help. You want to please him. Do you realize that most women wouldn't? They wouldn't care what he wanted, or they would have said that he just needed to get used to whatever they do, or they would ask their own mother, but you want to step into his world and make him feel comfortable. And that takes a certain amount of humility, and that's priceless."

"Well, everything you said is true about what I want. But it just seems like the normal thing to do."

"It might be, but not everyone does it." Marjorie nodded her head and then tapped her finger on the recipe book. "Your effort means more than anything."

The method Marjorie suggested worked perfectly, and Charity was able to sit in the car and make out a grocery list, and then go to the store and get the things she needed.

Before she had checked out, Wilson had sent her a text.

I didn't realize until after you're gone that it would make more sense for us to unload the groceries in my house. I'm sorry I didn't think of that earlier. Will you let me know what time I can meet you there, and I'll help you carry the stuff in? Mom is coming to stay with the kids.

I'm checking out now.

They arranged a time to meet, and for some reason, that made Charity nervous. She had been in his house a few times carrying things in as they moved, but even though she was supposed to be making his house her home, it felt...like she needed to ask before she touched anything. Plus, there hadn't been too many times where she and Wilson had been alone since they'd been married. Usually there were kids around almost constantly. At night, after she put the kids to bed, he always said good night to her at the top of the stairs and went back downstairs by himself. She supposed she could say something along the lines of, "I wasn't done downstairs, I'm coming back down with you," but she hadn't.

She hadn't been lying when she said it felt good to be able to trust that someone else was downstairs taking care of things, locking up, making sure the house was secure, and she didn't want him to think that she didn't appreciate that.

So, her hands sweated and her heart tripped as she pulled in the driveway to his farm and parked beside his truck at his house. He was already out of his truck, wearing a plaid button-down, leaning against the door, watching her pull in.

So handsome, and he looked so capable, so strong and self-assured, and she took a moment to admire him as she pulled in.

She should have backed in, but she didn't want to take a chance that she might back into his truck, since she was a pretty good driver going forward, but backward had never been her best direction.

"Sorry about the last-minute switch-up," he said as she pulled in and got out of her car, popping the trunk.

"It's okay. I'm glad you thought of it. Otherwise, we'd be moving all of this stuff tomorrow. Or we'd be here at your house with nothing to eat."

"I'm not sure what could be worse than having five children and no food."

"Having five children and a husband with no food?" she asked, gently teasing him for the amount of food he ate.

She thought his cheeks were getting red, but it was hard to tell since he let his beard grow out in the cooler weather. She liked it, quite a lot. She'd always loved a neatly trimmed beard, and his was just ragged enough to give him a rough-and-tumble look without making him look like the beard had taken over everything.

"I think the lady thinks I eat too much."

"The lady does not think you eat too much at all. The lady is happy to cook for people who like to eat." And that was the truth.

They gathered up bags and walked in together, with him opening the door and holding it with his foot so she could walk in first.

"There is a freezer downstairs that's mostly empty right now, but if we need any extra room, or if we'd like to butcher a half a beef, there's room to put it down there."

"Oh, that's nice. Do you eat your own?"

"I often do. If someone orders a half, and there's no one beating the door down for the other half, I might keep that for myself. Or split it out between my family members and others."

It was interesting the way he said others. Like who else would he share with, other than his family?

She didn't dwell on that long but walked beside him back out to the trunk to get more.

"I talked to your mom, and she gave me the recipes of the food that she thought you like the best. So, I bought all the ingredients for them. I considered that you might have your own meat, but you hadn't said, so I bought that too."

"I'm pretty much out right now. I think there are a few packages of hamburger in the freezer above the refrigerator, but I'm going to have a steer ready to take in another few weeks, and then we'll have all we can use."

"No chicken?"

"No. I buy that." He looked over at her. "You like chickens?"

"I guess I've always dreamed about having my own hens. It just seems so...fun."

"It's work too, but it probably would be good work for the kids. Although, obviously someone has to supervise."

"I'm not sure I'd want to let the kids do it. I'm pretty sure that's something I would like to do by myself for a while, unless I'm too tired."

He laughed, like the idea of her wanting to take care of her chickens rather than letting her kids do it was funny.

"We live on a farm now, so chickens are fine, and you have your own beef, and I suppose if you're really excited about it, you could get a milk cow. But that's even more work, because you have to milk her morning and night, so you really can't leave to go anywhere."

"I guess it would tie you down, but that would be so much fun." She wasn't being naïve. She knew it would be a lot of work. But the idea of having her own cow, her own chickens, meat they'd raised on the farm, were things that she'd just dreamed about before, and here he was casually making all of her dreams come true. Without even realizing it.

"The thing with cows versus chickens, if you go somewhere, it's not too hard to find someone who will at least make sure your chickens have water. You leave enough feed for them for a couple days, and they'll be fine. But a cow, on the other hand, if you're milking, it's kind of tough to find someone who is willing, and knows how, to milk a cow."

"I would have loved to have had someone ask me to milk their cow while they went on vacation. Of course, since I've never done it before, I might not have been able to. Is it hard?"

He laughed. "Not once you get the hang of it. I've seen people struggle with it for a while, just trying to get milk out. It takes a bit of a knack. For some cows too, it also takes hand strength. My grandma used to say that it was good for playing the piano, because it strengthened your hands. I don't know how true that is, because I don't think playing the piano really takes a lot of hand strength."

"Looks like it would be more arm strength and finger dexterity, but I don't know. I never had the opportunity to take lessons."

"My grandma wanted to give me lessons, and the rest of my family, but most of us didn't want to put the work into it. Because that's what it was, time away from playing with our friends, while we sat down on the piano bench and practiced because that's the only way she would give us lessons. Was if we spent half an hour every day practicing."

"Wow. I guess that's one way to learn, if you're forced to practice."

"Yeah, and who wants to do that rather than play?"

"Some kids don't have a choice. They just have to do it, like school."

"I think that's a good idea. To make kids learn to play an instrument. Just like we make them go to school. There are far worse things they could learn, and probably are learning, in school than to have to sit in a music class for half an hour a day practicing an instrument. In fact, I would say there aren't too many better things that they could be doing with their time."

"Can't say that I disagree with you on that one, and I kind of wish that's the way it would have been when I was going to school. But that ship has sailed for me."

"For me, too. But we can make the kids learn to play instruments if you want to."

They had carried the last load of groceries in and stood at the table, facing each other as he said that last statement, and she realized he was serious.

"Who would give the lessons?" And then she looked around. "I don't even have a piano."

"I have my grandmother's piano in here. So don't let that stop you." He ran a hand over his hair. "I don't know if I should be suggesting it though, when I didn't do it as a child even though I had the opportunity."

"I can't imagine a kid not wanting to learn to play the piano. I would have jumped on that with both hands if I would have had someone offering to give me lessons."

"I guess it's just different interests. Although, every once in a while, I regret not learning."

"So... Do you think it's worthwhile to make our kids do it?"

"I know that some people would say that you should allow the child to guide you and let them do what they're interested in, but there is a certain amount of discipline that it takes to learn to play, and it develops your character. I guess... If you're for it, I'm down for it too. Although, I'm not sure I'm down for all five of them learning at one time."

"That's two and a half hours of practicing each day. Two and a half hours of constant piano noise in the background."

Some days, it was all she could stand to listen to the kids chattering in the background, and by the time they went to bed, she was so ready for the peace and quiet she could hardly stand it.

"You're going to be the one who has to listen to it. Are you going to be okay with it?"

She couldn't believe that he was giving her the option. Just like he had given her his wallet.

"Oh! Here, before I forget." She took his wallet out of her pocket and handed it over.

"I wasn't sure if I was going to see that again or not."

"Really?" she asked, and they grinned at each other.

"It's yours anytime you want it. I guess we should talk about a budget and our expenses and that kind of thing, because I do kinda try to watch, but... It's not like we have to pinch pennies, because we don't."

"Well, if you tell me what the budget is and the expenses that we have, I am perfectly okay with it. I shouldn't have much of anything, since my car is paid for, and... The house is not, but if we sell it, then that's out of the picture, and there's nothing else other than insurance and the phone bill."

"We'll have two bills until we sell the house too, but yeah. We'll sit down sometime and talk about it. I didn't want to overwhelm you when we were first married. There are a lot of things for both of us to get used to. Combining a family isn't easy."

"You are the one who had to make the most adjustments. I was used to the constant noise and chaos of five children. It was probably a bit of a wake-up call for you."

"It just took me back to my childhood." He looked around the kitchen. "I think it's going to be really nice having that kind of noise in this old house. I got a little lonely, and it definitely seemed quiet at times."

"Sometimes I crave quiet," she admitted. And then figured she probably shouldn't, because it was going to be a long time until her life had any semblance of quietness in it again. A long time.

"I get that. I guess I'm more of an extrovert. But I think Terry especially sometimes was overwhelmed with all the noise in our house, because she's more of an introvert." He paused for a moment and then looked at the stuff on the table. "How about I show you where all this stuff goes? And then, you can rearrange the kitchen at your convenience. Actually, you can rearrange anything in the house if you want to. It's ours, not mine."

"I don't want to come in and upend everything that you've done."

"I want you to feel at home. And if that means that you need to rearrange some things, then that's the way it needs to be. I don't have anything that's so precious that it can't be moved. You're more important than anything I own."

He said it so casually as he grabbed some of the dry goods and started talking about where he put them in the cupboard. She followed along, listening, figuring that she probably wouldn't move anything to begin with and just try to get used to his system. But she appreciated his consideration, the fact that he made sure that she knew that she was more important, and while she supposed that some people might have just been saying that to sound good, she knew that Wilson actually meant it.

She thought again about what his mother had said about him being the golden child, the one that everything always came easily for, and who never really had to work for anything. Sometimes that could make a person spoiled, inconsiderate, assuming that everyone else should be as good as they were or there was some merit of their own which gave them their ability to turn things from nothing into a success. But Wilson seemed to have remained humble despite it all. Maybe it was whatever had gone down with his dad. She heard different people saying that that had been hard, and maybe that was what had forged his character into the strong, upright person he was today.

Whatever it was, she appreciated it and felt like she was benefiting more than she should have, as she usually did when she spent time with Wilson.

Would she ever feel like she deserved him? And better yet, would she ever feel like he wanted her as much as she wanted him?

Chapter Nineteen

"Wilson, Charity, come on in. Hey, guys." Marjorie opened the door and escorted his family into her house.

Wilson always loved coming back to visit. It seemed to make his mother extremely happy, and he loved the fact that his children had a good relationship with her. She didn't seem to care that they weren't really his, which he hated that idea, but it was there, and it was fact, and he supposed that he might as well stop fighting it.

"Hey, guys," Terry said as she and Judd got up from the living room and walked out to greet them.

"I didn't know you guys were here. I'm sorry we descended on you with our chaos." Wilson laughed as he pulled first one arm then another out of Evans's coat and hung it up by the door.

"I'm glad you're here. We don't get to see you nearly enough," Terry said. "I imagine that will change come summertime when we're all out and about a little bit more."

It was January 25, the one-month anniversary of Charity's and his marriage. He had a little surprise in his pocket, and he was hoping to be able to give it to her tonight after the kids went to bed.

He had been going to give it to her during naptime, but Serafina hadn't slept very well, and Charity had ended up lying down with her and falling asleep herself.

He hoped she was getting enough rest. He was concerned that maybe she was working herself too hard, but what else was a person supposed to expect from a mother of five children? Of course she was going to be working hard.

Terry came the rest of the way out and gave Charity a hug, who had just hung up Serafina's coat. "I'm so glad to see you. I am thrilled your children have been well and I haven't seen them in the practice, but every once in a while, I think, 'well, at least I would see my sister-in-law more if her kids were in here more.'"

They laughed together, and Charity said, "I'm so grateful we haven't been sick much this winter. It seemed like last winter all I did was sit on the couch and hold one of my kids who was crying because of an ear infection or they just felt miserable because they had a cold."

"I'm sure that wears on you."

"It does. And it seemed like Gifford missed a lot of school because of that, and I don't think we were in church the entire month of January."

"It's a good thing that this is a better year for you."

"I think we got immune to everything last year, so there isn't anything new to get thrown at us."

"Well, you have Wilson now, so at least you have someone to take turns sitting with you on the couch. And now that he's not doing the Secret Saint anymore, he has even more time."

Wilson froze, and his eyes shot to Charity. He had never told her about being the Secret Saint.

Charity's eyes got big, and it didn't take Terry long to read her expression and know that she hadn't known. Charity looked at Wilson, who didn't know what to say. This wasn't really the time or place for him to explain what exactly he had done, and before he could say anything, Terry put her hand over her mouth.

"I am so sorry. I just assumed... But I shouldn't have. Wilson. I really didn't mean anything by that." She sounded horrified and extremely upset, but Wilson shook his head.

"Don't worry about it. I should have told her. It's my fault for not. I just...quit and didn't consider talking about it again. Totally my fault."

"No, I should have kept my big mouth shut. I'm usually pretty good at that, but I messed up."

"Terry. I promise. It's not a big deal." He said that, and he meant it, but Charity looked like it was an extremely big deal, and he thought again about the little surprise that was in his pocket, the thing that he finally got around to getting, and he had expected today to be a special day, because of it being their one-month anniversary and all that, but it seemed like Charity might be taking this way out of context, except she wasn't. Not really. He hadn't told her, and he owed it to her for her to know, as his wife, what he was up to.

Except he wasn't doing it anymore. But she would know that he was the one who had spearheaded the groceries that they had gotten before Christmas and the gifts under the tree, and she might even wonder...if he had taken the Secret Saint thing a little bit too far and married her.

Yeah. She would wonder that. She wouldn't know that that had nothing to do with him being the Secret Saint and everything to do with him wanting to. He had already explained that to her, how he felt like it was what God wanted, and then he realized that it was really something that he wanted to do, too.

God couldn't have given him a better woman.

From the expression on Charity's face, she wasn't seeing it like that at all.

They had moved into the dining room, and his mom had set her French onion chicken casserole on the table. It was one of his favorites, and Charity had made it several times. It tasted better than his mom's when she made it. And he told her so. He tried as hard as he could to think about what a man would do to show he cared for his wife, and to treat Charity that way. But maybe he wasn't doing a very good job. Obviously from that horrified look on her face, he'd screwed up in that area at least. And maybe, maybe if she liked and respected him a little bit more, and trusted him, she wouldn't look so horrified.

Chapter Twenty

"Good night, Mommy," Lavinia said.

Charity swallowed before she replied, "Good night, Lavinia."

She walked out of the door, breathing a sigh of relief. She had held up rather well, she thought, considering that she had a pretty huge shock at the beginning of the evening.

She and Wilson had been married a month. She'd woken up smiling over their anniversary, although still frustrated because their relationship seemed to be going nowhere. He still slept downstairs on the couch, only on his couch now that they'd moved, and she slept upstairs in the room that used to be his bedroom but now was solely hers.

She supposed this was what she got for agreeing to a marriage of convenience. Although, she couldn't blame it all on that. It was very difficult to find time alone without the children. They got up early, and while they didn't go to bed super late, by the time she got them in bed and tucked in with all the stories and drinks and bathroom runs and changes of clothes and baths, she was exhausted. She assumed Wilson was the same.

She just couldn't wait to go into her room, close the door, and try to process what she learned tonight.

"I was hoping I could talk to you for a few minutes." Wilson's voice came down the hall, and she turned, not seeing him there at the top of the steps in the dark.

"Of course," she said. She wasn't mad at him. Not really. She was more mad at herself. For being so stupid. Hoping that they would have something more than just a friendly relationship; she should have known better. She didn't even know what she wanted.

She just knew that she wasn't expecting to hear that Wilson was the one who had made sure that her children had gifts and who made sure that she had money for groceries and who had brought her electric bill current so that her lights didn't get turned off. It was embarrassing, of course, but more than that, she felt betrayed, because she hadn't known. Wasn't him marrying her taking the Secret Saint thing a little bit too far? Why hadn't he said anything? Surely he could have told her, "Hey, I've been doing some nice things for you, one more nice thing I'd like to do is to marry you."

Of course he couldn't say that.

"Today is one month since we got married," he said softly.

"I know. I woke up thinking about it, but then the kids got up, and I never said anything to you. But happy anniversary."

It was like a teenager, who celebrated the anniversary of going out with her boyfriend, except she was married. And she didn't know her husband any better than a teenager might know that boy she was dating. Less probably.

"I got you something. I am a little nervous, because I wasn't sure whether you'd like it. And actually there's something in there for me too." He handed her a little box. It was a jewelry box, and her heart stirred while her hand went to her mouth.

"Aren't you going to open it? Are you going to leave me here nervously wiping my hands on my jeans and praying that you like it indefinitely?"

"You're nervous," she said, smiling up at him.

"Yes. I thought long and hard about this, and I almost took you with me to pick them out, but I wanted it to be a surprise. You don't get too many of those."

She didn't. But she'd had a different surprise tonight. One that wasn't nearly as good. She needed to talk to him about it, but she didn't want to ruin this moment. He was making it so sweet.

Admitting that he was nervous, wanting her to like it, wanting her to have a surprise. She really couldn't complain about any of it. In fact, it was also very considerate of him.

She slowly opened the lid of the box, savoring the idea of a gift. They hadn't exchanged gifts at Christmas. She hadn't even known that he was going to be in her life, when she had thought about shopping, not that she had any money to buy anything.

And she assumed the same was true for him, since there had been a gift from the Secret Saint saying...that had been him. She shook her head, and then pushed the thought aside. She'd take that up with him in a minute, but first, she wanted to appreciate whatever it was that he had gotten her.

He said there was something in there for him, and so when she opened it and saw a set of wedding rings, she wasn't exactly surprised. But the diamond ring that winked beside them just threw her a bit.

"Wow," she breathed, touching them gently with her finger, like they were going to feel like anything other than cold metal and stone.

"I ask your friend Kyra what your finger size was. She didn't know, but she took her best guess. They might not fit, but the jeweler said he could resize them."

"Oh. I... I wanted a ring, but I hated to ask, because... It seemed frivolous with all the other things, and that's something that you never even talked about—the expense of taking on five children and a wife. Your grocery bill might only have doubled, but there are so many other things that have to be bought. I'm sorry."

"It's what I want to spend my money on. Trust me. I thought

long and hard about it, and I couldn't think of anything more worthy."

"I wanted to talk to you about that."

She looked up at him, and he seemed to know what she meant because he nodded, and then he said, "Want to see if the rings fit first?"

The thought went through her head that maybe he was giving her the rings to butter her up because he knew that there was going to be a confrontation, but she shook the thought aside immediately. Of course he wasn't doing that. He couldn't have gone to the store and bought the rings after he heard her finding out about him being the Secret Saint. And she believed him when he said he wanted to do it to celebrate their wedding anniversary.

It all made total sense, and she needed to just accept his words at face value. After all, she wanted him to accept her words the same.

He had gotten her ring out first, the diamond. It wasn't huge, but it sparkled in the light and was nicer than anything she ever had, including the diamond ring that she sold once her husband had left her. It had bought groceries for a week.

She didn't get nearly what they had paid for it, but groceries had been more important than rings at that point in her life.

"It fits perfectly." She held her hand up, admiring the way the band looked on her finger.

"I'm pretty sure the diamond goes on first? Or is it the wedding band?"

"I think the wedding band goes on first." She really wasn't up on all those things, but that was the way she had always seen them.

"Then, here, take that off for a second and let me slip this on first. They should look good together, because they were a set."

He didn't say anything else as she slipped the diamond ring off, and he slid the wedding band on her finger.

She went to put the diamond ring back on, but his hands met hers and he grasped the ring in her fingers. "May I?"

"Of course," she said.

"With this ring, I thee wed. Forsaking all others, I pledge my life to you, until death do us part." He spoke the words as he slid the ring on her finger, similar to the vows they'd spoken at their wedding, but these came from his heart.

They made tears prick in her eyes. She swallowed hard, staring down at her hand but not seeing it. He'd been better to her than anyone in her life had ever been. He treated her well, had stood by her, even when her kids had been a disaster, had chosen to marry her when his life would have been so much easier if he hadn't. Had taken her children as his own. Had given her everything she needed, and told her that whatever was his was hers too. He hadn't said a word when she rearranged a few things in the kitchen and had gladly given up his bedroom so that she could have it while he slept on the couch.

"They're perfect," she said with a slight tremble in her voice, but she looked up and smiled at him to let him know that there was nothing wrong. "Can I put yours on?"

He nodded.

She took the ring, fingering it for a moment, knowing it would fit because he had bought it, and wanting to do the same for him that he had done for her.

She took his hand and slid the ring over his finger, wriggling it a bit as it got stuck on his knuckle. "With this ring, I thee wed. I pledge my life to you, in sickness and in health, until death do us part."

The light in the hall was bright enough for her to see his teeth glint as he smiled. Maybe she held his hand a bit too long, but somehow their fingers twined together, and he turned a little, and she took a step closer, his free hand coming up and pushing back the hair away from her temple as his lips came down and he touched them to her forehead.

"Thank you," he whispered, and she didn't know why he was thanking her.

"It's me that should be thanking you. These rings are beautiful. I'm honored to wear them."

"No. Thank you for pledging your life to me. A good woman is rather to be had than great riches. You're worth more than any material things to me. You, and your children, our children, have filled a spot in my life I didn't even know was empty. I just wanted to thank you."

Maybe that was what the rings were. A thank you for all the things he just said.

She hadn't gotten a chance to try to figure it out or unentangle it and explain to him that she was the one who was grateful, and he said when he pulled back a bit, "I wanted to apologize for the way you found out about the Secret Saint tonight."

It all came rushing back, the betrayal, the clenching of her chest as she realized that maybe he hadn't lied to her, but he had definitely kept something from her that was rather important.

She didn't say anything, but involuntarily her fingers clenched around his.

His hand came up and gently pushed her hair back again, trailing his fingers through it, and maybe if she had been able to form a coherent thought, she would have noticed that he seemed to enjoy the way her hair felt against his fingers as they moved slowly down, allowing the strands to slide through.

"I know that wasn't good. I just wanted you to know that I didn't mean anything by it. I quit doing it after I saw you, your children, the difficult things you had been through, and found out your story. That's when God clearly told me that what I was doing as a Secret Saint wasn't what I was supposed to be doing. And I've mentioned this before, but I don't think it was necessarily to help you. I think God knew that I needed you. I needed your children. It was for me. Not you."

Her eyes widened as he spoke in the dim light, saying words she wasn't expecting to hear.

"I thought maybe marrying me was just an extension of the Secret Saint. Taking it a little bit too far."

"No. I promise you. I've never lied to you. Everything I've said has been the absolute truth. I know it looks bad that I didn't tell you about it, but I was done with it. I had given it up. I wasn't doing it anymore because I knew I couldn't do that and take care of my family. And this is where I'm supposed to be. Right here, with you."

That wasn't what she was expecting to hear, but it was exactly what she needed to hear. Everything he said was exactly right. She just hoped it was the truth. Because if it was, it was exactly the right thing for him to do and say.

"You gave up a lot for me."

"I gained more," he said softly.

She nodded, although she didn't necessarily agree. She didn't really see it that way. She saw someone who was good at everything being benevolent, and maybe giving up his opportunity to fall in love on his own, and being saddled with someone he didn't choose. Except he really did choose her.

"The rings are beautiful. Thank you so much," she finally said, looking up at him, not knowing what else to say.

"I wanted you to have them. Not just for you, but because when people look at you, I want them to know that you belong to me." He held up his hand, letting go of hers, as he flashed his ring at her. "And I belong to you."

That was really the way it was supposed to be. She knew that some people bristled at the idea of belonging. Like they were a possession, but that was really what marriage was, forsaking all others and belonging solely to the one to whom you pledged your life. You had a person who was totally and completely devoted to you.

Unless they cheated. Which hurt more than words can say. Maybe that was why she had such a hard time believing Wilson. Because Clancy had said the same vows, and he was supposed to belong to her, except he shared himself, without her knowledge, with others. In fact, he ditched her and told her he didn't want her anymore. Treated her like yesterday's news. Sadly.

"All right. I don't want to keep you any longer. I know it's been a big day, but I wanted to celebrate our anniversary. It's the first of many, I hope, and I just wanted you to have that, the rings, and I'll let you go."

"All right. Thank you. I...don't have anything for you." She remembered that wasn't the first gift he'd given. If he was the Secret Saint, there had been a gift for her under the tree as well.

He had started to move away, going down the steps, but she needed to thank him for that.

"Wilson?"

"Yeah?" he asked, his hand on the banister, stopping abruptly as soon as she spoke his name.

"Thank you for the candle you gave me for Christmas. I didn't know it was you."

He smiled a bit. "I didn't usually pick out things myself, but I did get that. With a little help from my mom and my sisters who have children and know what it's like, and they said that that would be something that you might appreciate."

"It is. Thank you. I just realized that these rings aren't the first gift you've given me."

"I enjoy giving you gifts. I hope it's okay."

"I don't know what to get for you. It seems like you have everything."

"Now that I have you, I do," he said softly, and then, pausing for just a moment, he turned and went the rest of the way down the stairs.

His words hung in the air as she turned back to his room. They were sweet, and she believed he truly meant them. The problem was she wanted to give him something physical, something tangible, but she couldn't think of anything, and even if she could, she had to use his money to purchase it, which kind of defeated the purpose. Maybe, now that they were moved in and settled, they could work on getting her baking business up and running. There was a small shed with electricity near the house, which he had said she could use to make her baked goods in. She had to get to work on that.

Chapter Twenty-One

February 25

"How does it look?" Wilson asked as Charity grabbed his hand and led him out to the shed that she'd been working on every chance she got. Which was mostly when he was able to get inside and watch the kids so that she could go out. And during naptime too.

"I think it's ready."

"I think someone's a little excited," he said, grabbing a hold of the baby monitor that usually sat on the counter, so he could take it with him in case Evans got up before they got back in.

Evans had been crawling out of his crib lately, which was fine as long as someone was in the house, but he didn't want Evans running around the house without any adult supervision. He wasn't quite old enough to know not to put things in the electrical sockets, and he also had never gone down the stairs by himself without someone standing with him to make sure he didn't fall.

"I know this isn't going to be so exciting for you, but it's all ready, and I even called the grocery store, the one that Ray Zigler manages, and he put in a huge order for next week. So I already have a business!"

He wasn't sure he'd ever seen Charity quite that excited. She was practically levitating as they went out and walked across the yard, all but dragging him to the door to her shed.

There weren't any windows in it, other than one which overlooked the yard. She'd be able to watch the kids from that window anyway.

But as he stepped in, he looked around and whistled.

"You have scrubbed this thing from top to bottom." And then his eyes landed on the stove. "I didn't even know what color that old thing was."

"I didn't either. And lo and behold, it's white!" she said, laughing as she let go of his hand enough to clap, putting her hands underneath her chin and looking at him. "What do you think?"

"I think it's going to pass inspection."

"I was hoping you would say that. They're supposed to come tomorrow. That's why I've been working so hard to get it done. But I have everything scrubbed as good as I can get it, and if they're going to find fault with anything, it's not going to be something that I could have done myself."

He smiled at the excitement in her eyes and the anticipation that she showed. It was obvious she was looking forward to it. He was a little bit jealous that she didn't show that kind of excitement about him. That kind of...desire, he supposed that was the word he wanted. Maybe attraction. But she definitely was excited about her baking and not excited about her husband. Although he was the one she wanted to show it to. So there was that. But he would rather she worked on their relationship than put all of her energy into this baking business that she had had before and wanted again.

"Can I ask a question?" he asked, figuring that that was about the stupidest question a person could ask but not knowing how else to approach the subject. He had told her that if he had an issue, he would always say something.

"Of course you can!" she said, grinning at him. And obviously expecting him to ask her something about her baking business. He supposed he was.

"Is there a reason you're so excited to...put more work on your plate? I mean, is there something that's more fulfilling about baking for other people?" He hoped that didn't sound terrible. He didn't mean to insult her, he just didn't understand why...why she couldn't be that happy to be with him. Why she had to look outside of their marriage and relationship in order to be fulfilled. He loved farming, but he would give it up in a heartbeat if he had to for his family. Even for the kids that were not biologically his. They felt like they were his in every other way.

She tilted her head, looking at him, knowing him well enough to know that he wasn't insulting her, and he appreciated that. Maybe over the last month, she had learned to trust him a little.

"I guess I'm more excited about being able to pull my weight around here than I am about actually doing the work. You know? Like I'm not going to be this thing that is hanging over your head and just costing you money. I'll be able to contribute to the family as well. That makes me happy."

"But you are contributing. You take care of everyone, including me. You cook, you clean, you work from the time you get up in the morning until you go to bed at night, and you never stop. I really don't know how you're going to fit the baking into your schedule, not that I don't want you to, because I do. I just was hoping you'd help me understand why it means so much to you so that it makes more sense to me. Because all I see is you taking on more work, and I'm already trying to figure out how to get you to do less, not more."

He held his breath, because he figured that there were some women who would have exploded over what he had just said. But Charity didn't.

"But there's no money in that stuff. And I feel bad that instead of you just taking care of you, you're taking care of us."

"I've spent my money on other people. It was satisfying, but now I'm spending it on my family, and that's even better."

The light dawned in her eyes a little, and he knew she understood he was talking about the work that he had done for the Secret Saint.

"Do you see that it will be satisfying for me to have money to spend on my family?"

"So it's not enough for me to take care of you?"

The words hung in the air between them, and he could see her trying not to be upset.

He didn't want to have a fight. Not today. It was their two-month anniversary. Normally he didn't pay any attention to such things, but he'd been looking forward to the day. Even watching the calendar, and watching as she cleaned, and realizing that she was going to be done on this day, and seeing that was fitting. But he supposed that he was letting her know that it was hurting him a little bit, just the fact that she wasn't content to just let him take care of them, but she wanted to do something too.

"I suppose I need to be okay with the fact that while I want to be the one to take care of you, you want to be able to contribute to our household too. And we can't have it both ways, so one of us has to give. Right?"

The excitement had drained from her eyes, and she nodded slowly. "I hadn't thought about it like that. I guess... If that's the way you feel about it. This is what I want to do."

He shook his head, even though he closed his eyes and prayed for a second, asking the Lord what he had done wrong. Why had he even opened his mouth? Because he had wanted to voice the issues that he was having. But he hadn't wanted her to give up anything.

"No. That wasn't what I wanted at all. I guess I just didn't understand that you wanted to be able to contribute to the household too. I... It's not about me, but you're not saying that I'm not enough. You're saying that you want to join me, and we'll do this together?"

Her lips curved up in a tentative smile. "Yeah. That's exactly it. I... I wanted to get you a gift, but for me to use your money to buy you a gift seems silly. You know?"

"It's not my money, it's our money. That's the way I see it, anyway."

"I see it that way too. Except when you look at the root of the situation, the money came from you. I want to earn my own money, and yeah, so that you and I can work together, so we'll be a team, but also so that if I want to get you something, it's not coming from you to you, it's coming from me, which makes a difference to me. Does that make sense?"

He nodded. He was mostly okay, hearing her explain it, glad he'd brought it up, and she hadn't got mad and stormed off saying, "Fine, I won't do it after all if that's not what you want." Which she could have.

"Thanks for taking the time to listen and think about it. I... I wanted to talk to you about it, but I was afraid that you would get mad at me. And you could have. A lot of people would have."

"Yeah. I guess I felt a little hurt when we started talking, but I think I see what you're saying. And I think you understand my point of view, and I'm still willing to not do it if that's what you want."

"No. If this makes you happy, I want you to have it."

She stared at him, as though she wasn't quite sure whether he was being serious or not. "I suppose the only thing that the Bible says about it is that the man provides, and he is the head of home, so if you say I can't, then I won't, and you know I won't be upset about it. Because you're in charge. But if you say I can, then I'm going to, unless that's going to upset you and we're going to fight about it. Because getting along with you is more important to me than having this between us."

"Yes. Having a good relationship with you is far more important to me than whether or not you do baked goods. I love that you do them, I love that you make money on it, and I guess it might take me a little bit to get used to the idea that we're doing this together, and I'm not the only one providing."

"Aren't we doing it together anyway? I mean, we do the kids together, and you told me in the spring when things start picking up on the farm, I'm going to be helping you with that, more than just feeding the cows."

He'd taken her out some to feed the animals, but there wasn't enough room in the tractor for all six of them to ride together, so the few times he'd taken her out had been when his mom had come and watched the kids.

"You're right. I was expecting you to work on the farm. And I suppose that in a way, you're contributing in that regard anyway." He sighed. "Please be happy and excited again, and I'm sorry I said anything that drained your enthusiasm, because I really enjoyed seeing how happy you were, and I just wanted to understand it."

"Yeah. I'm sorry. I guess... I guess it is kind of a mystery. I can see how it would be anyway. And... Thank you for saying something rather than just getting mad at me and telling me I couldn't do it. I think that's what Clancy would have done, and I appreciate you having a conversation, even if it was kind of hard for you, and I really appreciate you being willing to capitulate even though maybe you don't quite get it completely."

He grinned. She'd figured out that he still wasn't quite all in, but she had the confidence that he would get there. He had the confidence too. Sometimes it just took him a little while.

"Do you promise me that if this keeps being a problem for you, you'll say something?" she asked, and then she grinned engagingly. "Since you know that I'm not going to get mad and storm off?"

He laughed. "Good point. Probably if you did get mad, it would make me hesitate to say anything, and that's just asking for trouble, when you let things go until you're so mad you want to explode."

"Well, I've never seen you explode. It's kind of hard for me to picture that, but I'll take your word for it."

"Trust me, I'm sure it could happen to anyone. Although you're pretty even-keeled too. So maybe we inspire each other to keep our explosions to a minimum."

They grinned at each other, and then he took another look around, admiring how she had made the little shack into a cozy bakery that sparkled with cleanliness and oozed with the idea that something yummy could come out of it.

"I'm so proud of what you did here. It is pretty amazing. We should have before and after pictures."

"I do!" she said, grinning again.

He could hardly take his gaze off her. Her eyes were shining and her cheeks were bright and she looked so happy and carefree, and so much younger than the tired, worn-out mom of five that he had married just two months ago.

"Hey, happy anniversary," he said as he held his hand out to her, and she put her fingers in his, and they slid together.

"Happy anniversary. I can't imagine being any happier than I am right now."

"I can't imagine admiring you any more than I do right now," he said, and his words surprised her, as she widened her eyes. He didn't give her a chance to say anything more but squeezed her hand, as the monitor crackled with the baby's crying, and they walked out of the shed hand in hand, together.

Chapter Twenty-Two

March 25

"Are you sure you're going to be okay?" Charity asked for what felt like the hundredth time. Marjorie smiled benignly, as though Charity could ask her a million times and Marjorie would still give her the same patient answer.

"We'll be fine, won't we, children?" she asked as she looked around the table at the kids who sat eating their breakfast as she helped feed Evans who sat in his high chair.

"We get to spend the day with Grandma!" Banks called out, grinning and smiling and looking excited.

"I'm not jealous about that," she murmured as they waved to Marjorie and Wilson and she walked out of the kitchen.

"It is a little disheartening, isn't it? We work our butts off to give them good lives, and they're okay with it, but Grandma comes, and they go wild with excitement."

"Probably because she's going to play the quiet game," Charity said with a wink at Wilson.

He chuckled with her and opened her side of the pickup so she could get in.

Even when they had children, he always opened her door for her. He said that he wanted to set a good example for his boys. To show them that women deserve consideration and respect.

She watched as he walked around the front of the vehicle. So many people said that when a man was the head of the home, the woman was automatically in subjection and couldn't live her best life or whatever, but after spending several months with Wilson, Charity was sure that it was all in how seriously a man took his duty to treat the woman the way Christ treated the church and gave himself for it.

She never felt like she was less than. And the conversation that they'd had a month ago when she opened her business haunted her, but she didn't think it was because he didn't want her to earn money, or because he didn't want her to have a business. But she couldn't quite put her finger on what it was. She had the feeling that it was something that he was a little bit ashamed of and didn't want to talk to her about. Even though he said he wanted to be able to talk to her about anything. It seemed like he had tried but hadn't quite been able to get everything out that he needed to say.

Maybe she was just making stuff up. Maybe there really wasn't any problem, and it was in her head.

"Are you going to tell me where we're going?" she asked as he put the car in reverse and pulled out of the drive.

He had fed the cows early and made sure she didn't have any last-minute baking to do, so they could have the whole day together.

Both of them knew it was their anniversary, and they'd greeted each other with "happy anniversary" that morning. It was funny that they were keeping track, and every month they marked it.

She was sure after they had been married for a few years, or maybe it would not even be that long, it would be old hat, but their relationship was new. And she appreciated the fact that Wilson was trying to make it...romantic, maybe?

She wasn't exactly sure, but whatever the effort was for, she appreciated it.

"Don't you want to guess?" he asked, grinning at her as though they shared a silent joke. Banks was in the stage where he wanted people to guess everything, whether it was what he was doing next, or what he had already done, or how his day was, the standard answer was "guess!"

"I really have no idea. I mean, it has to be somewhere within a day's ride, because we have to make it back today. Your mom didn't bring an overnight bag."

"You're right about that. We're not going more than half a day's ride away."

"And I'm guessing that we're going to eat, since we skipped out on breakfast and I'm starving and you have to be practically dying, because you fed the cows and haven't had anything to eat since you got up."

"You're right. I'm pretty hungry." He shot her a grin but then put his eyes right back on the road.

"And we're going down the mountain, so it's something that is in this direction."

"That's correct. I'm not trying to confuse you by taking the long way."

"All right. But beyond that, I really have no idea. An auction?"

"Would you enjoy that?" he asked, sounding surprised.

"If I'm with you," she said easily, remembering how much it had meant to her when he had said that he wanted to be with her.

Her words made him smile. "Try again."

"Out to eat?"

"We're going to eat. But we're going to do something else."

"Man, I don't know. I'd say a riverboat cruise, but I don't think there are any riverboat cruises around here, and I'm honestly not sure they're even a thing."

"I think it might be a thing, but you're right. If they're around here, I've never heard of them. But that's close."

"Is it close enough for you to tell me?"

"Really? You don't want it to be a surprise?"

"I want to look forward to it! That's part of the fun."

"All right. I have tickets for the Blue Ridge train tour. They're going to feed us, take us for a ride, and I think as they're turning the train around, there's a lookout with a great view and information about the Virginia Railway or something like that."

"Wow. I've never even heard of that. But hey, if I get food, it sounds fun."

"It sounded good. I read the reviews, to make sure that people weren't complaining about it, because I know how much you love it when someone else feeds you. It would be pretty disappointing if the food ended up not being very good."

"I appreciate that," she said, feeling happy that he had remembered something that meant so much to her.

"It seems like your business is going really well, but you haven't talked about it lately, so I figured I'd ask."

"It's going great. I have orders almost every day. And I guess I haven't mentioned it because I know that you weren't completely all for it, and I wasn't quite sure what the issue was."

"You know, I wasn't quite sure what my issue was, either. I just don't allow it to bother me. I never did figure it out for the most part."

He didn't look away from the road, and she felt like he was telling her something that maybe he was a little bit ashamed of or embarrassed about.

"Okay?" she asked, waiting.

"I was jealous."

"Jealous?" she asked, shocked and trying to make sense of his answer.

"Yeah. And I know that sounds really weird, but you were so excited about it and happy, and I guess it bothered me the same way the kids did today when Mom comes in and they all act like she's the best thing that ever happened to them, and we're just here, slaving away every day all day long trying to keep a roof over their heads and keep them fed and alive, and they act like Mom's Superman or something."

"I see," she said, and she really did. He was jealous because she was excited about her business, but she hadn't shown the same excitement for him.

"Is that all you're gonna say?" he said, blinking his eyes over at her, a self-deprecating grin on his face.

"No. I guess not. I'm trying to figure out how to say that you mean more to me than the business does, and you're right, I did kind of act like the kids, but I wasn't jealous or anything of your mom because I know that they love her, and that makes me happy, and also I know that they love me, and eventually if Grandma was with them all the time, they would act that way when I showed up. But deep down, I know they love me."

"I guess that's what I finally reasoned out, that I was being silly to be jealous of you doing something and not seeming excited about me. It was pretty much the same. I knew you really liked me."

He didn't use the word "love," and she didn't miss that. But she didn't correct him either, because she wasn't going to tell him that she loved him. But she had been kind of feeling like she did love him. Not maybe the way the world saw love, although there were some odd feelings stirring in her chest every time he was around that made her feel like maybe there was some attraction. The problem was, she didn't feel like he was attracted to her. So it was hard for her to admit that. Still, she was pretty sure she could tell him that she loved him and it would be an honest thing. But maybe she had just been so set on showing him that she got caught up in it and hadn't thought about saying the words.

Not today though. She wasn't going to make today awkward. Not any more than she already had with her questions.

"That's the right conclusion," she finally said. "And I'm sorry that I hurt your feelings, I really didn't mean to. I guess... I guess you're right. I hate to say that I took you for granted. Especially after what my first husband did. I would like to think that I'll always appreciate someone who's kind to me, but in reality, I guess I've already messed that up."

"As I'm sure I've taken advantage of you, too. And taken you for granted. But that's kind of the point of remembering our anniversary. It's just kind of a reset every month for me to be like, 'hey, do something nice for your wife, because you know you want to.'" He put a hand up. "I don't want you thinking that I have to force myself to be nice to you. That's not it at all. Just sometimes... You get put on the back burner because there are other fires that demand attention, and you're content, even if you don't get everything that you probably should as my wife."

"I get more than I deserve."

They grinned at each other and kept chatting until they reached the train station, right on time, as the train was being loaded as they pulled in.

"We better hurry out, that train has my dinner on it," Wilson said as he opened her door and helped her out.

They held hands as they walked across the parking lot. Wilson showed the conductor their tickets, and they got on and found their seats.

The ride went by quickly, and before Charity knew it, several hours had slipped past, hours which she had spent laughing and enjoying the company of her husband.

Just before the train reached the station, she excused herself from the table to go back and use the restroom. As she was walking back between the tables, an older lady caught her hand.

"You two look so cute together. I've been enjoying this entire day just watching you two enjoy each other. I hope you know you have something special."

"I know I do. He's amazing."

"I meant between the two of you, but you're right, he's amazing, but you are too."

The old lady patted her hand, and Charity took that as her cue to continue on. But the lady had reminded her that it wasn't every day that someone had what she had with Wilson.

Could that be this elusive thing that everyone else got married for? That they looked for when they got married? Had they developed that after marriage?

Was that possible?

She had hoped and prayed that her husband would find her attractive, but she hadn't thought that they would have that special, soul-deep bond that made someone feel like they married their soulmate. Was that contrived? Could people develop it over time, even if they didn't think they were in love to begin with?

That went so far against everything that she had been brought up to believe that it was hard to grasp at first, but unless she and Wilson just lucked into each other, which she didn't believe for one second, it seemed like it was something that could develop if both people were focused on living for the other and being kind.

She made her way back and didn't see the lady sitting there, but she didn't think much more about it, other than to remind herself that she wanted to thank Wilson for being such a sweet date. She supposed that's what this was, a date.

"So was it a good anniversary?" Wilson said after they had disembarked from the train and he helped her into the pickup.

"The best. Although, I don't know. Every anniversary has been good so far."

"This is only the third one. Hopefully they get better from here."

"I feel kinda bad though, because it's always you doing stuff for me. You should let me plan our next anniversary."

"I can't do that, because I already have something in mind."

"Are you serious?" she asked, knowing that that anniversary was a full month away, and he already had plans for it? He really knew how to make her feel special.

"I sure do, and I'm looking forward to it, because I know you're gonna love it. And that's all you're going to get me to say," he said, giving her a nod and a smile before he shut the door.

She wasn't going to try to get it out of him. But she had a whole month to look forward to it, which was kind of nice.

"And just so you're aware, it's a lot of fun for me to do fun things for you, and I don't need anything in return, just your laughter and your smile and getting to spend the day with you and be in your company is more than enough. Not to say that to be sappy, I mean it." He sat down, closing the door and putting his seat belt on.

"You know what I mean?" he asked as he started the truck.

"I do. But you made me feel spoiled. In a really good way."

"Good. That's how I want you to feel. Like you have a husband who thinks the world of you."

That's exactly how she felt.

Chapter Twenty-Three

April 25

"How's married life treating you?" Kyra said as Charity walked around the kitchen getting breakfast ready. The post office had called at six o'clock that morning to let them know there was a package in for them, and for some reason, Wilson had taken the three older kids with him. Charity had no idea what the package was, probably a tractor part or a piece for the barn addition he had been building all winter.

"It's great. I mean, better than I ever dreamed. I am so glad I didn't let myself be influenced by my first marriage. Or I would have never got married again."

"What's it been? Almost four months?"

Charity's eyes widened. "Is it the twenty-fifth?"

"It is. Of April."

"Yeah. Exactly four months." She had almost forgotten their anniversary! But Wilson must've forgotten too, since he hadn't talked about doing anything that day, and they always greeted each other with "happy anniversary" on their anniversary, but he'd been so busy gathering up the kids to take them into the post office with him that he hadn't even said anything. It was the first anniversary that they'd almost forgotten, although Charity laughed at herself. It wasn't even seven o'clock in the morning. She wasn't close to forgetting it.

"Congratulations. You know there are some marriages that don't even last that long."

"I know. That's sad." She shuddered. Her first marriage had lasted longer than that, but it hadn't been a good one. Now that she knew what a good marriage was, she couldn't believe how long she'd been in a miserable one. But she had her children, and God had blessed her with a really great man.

"Are you ready for your spring program?" Kyra was involved in the new playhouse that had just opened in Mistletoe Meadows. She was part of the orchestra, and she loved it.

"I am. I can't wait. It's going to be so much fun. I think everyone feels that way. No one really cares that we're not getting paid a whole lot, you know?"

"In a small town like this, you really can't expect that there's going to be much of a crowd for everyone to make a killing, but who knows, maybe word will spread, and people will come."

"That's my dream. I mean, it's one of those dreams that I'm not afraid to dream even though I know it's probably not going to come true."

"You can see what happened to me, a single mom of five children who ended up with the most wonderful man in the world, and it is nothing short of a miracle. If that happened to me, anything could happen to anybody. You never know what God will do."

"You are an inspiration to me. No offense."

Charity laughed. She didn't take offense. She knew that it was true. Her situation had looked hopeless and had gotten completely turned around. If that was inspiration for people, then so be it. And she was glad of it.

"All right, I better go. I want to get some practice in before work."

"All right. Thanks for calling."

"Happy anniversary."

They hung up, and Charity hummed as she moved about the kitchen, thinking that she would have breakfast ready before they got home. She had been going to make eggs, but they only had six left, and that wasn't nearly enough to feed her family. Maybe someday she'd have hens of her own. Wilson had told her she could, but she figured that that probably got pushed aside because of all the other things he was doing, like putting the addition onto the barn, and today they were going to go to the sale barn.

She really couldn't be happier, unless she thought about how much she wanted her husband to want her, as a person, not just as a wife and mother. She couldn't explain it exactly. She just wanted him to be attracted to her, to give her little touches during the day, or hold her close at night, rather than escaping to the couch, while she felt stuck upstairs like that was his alone time and she didn't dare intrude upon it.

Not that he had ever said that, that was just the way she felt when they parted at the top of the stairs each night. That he was going to have time for himself, while she went to her lonely bedroom and slept alone. But she had determined that she would follow his lead, and she wasn't going to push him into something that he didn't want. If that was the kind of relationship that he wanted, then that would be what she would give him. Because he had given her so much more.

She got the oatmeal out and was stirring blueberries into it when the door burst open.

"Mommy! Mommy! You've got to come see this!"

Banks and Lavinia stood in the doorway, looking excited and like they could barely contain themselves.

"Is everyone okay?" she said, quickly turning the stove off and pulling the oatmeal off the burner.

"Mom, you have to see!"

"Mr. Wilson said that we can't tell you, you just have to come."

Maybe he hadn't forgotten their anniversary after all. Although, as excited as the kids were, she still worried that maybe there was something wrong.

"I'm coming. Where we going?"

"Out to the truck."

As she walked out the door, she saw her husband grinning, standing beside his truck, holding a brown box with little holes in it. Like air holes. It might be the kind of box in which a person would transport animals.

"What kind of animal did he get?"

Banks had a hold of one hand, Lavinia had a hold of the other, and they were both chattering at her side, or she might have heard the chicks chirping before she was standing right next to Wilson.

"Oh my goodness," she said, putting her hand to her chest. "You would not believe that I was just standing in the kitchen wishing that we had chickens because I don't have enough eggs to do breakfast."

"We should have more than enough eggs to do breakfast now, because you have fifteen Rhode Island Red hens in here."

"Just hens?" she asked, crunching up her brows. "Don't you need a rooster to have eggs?"

He chuckled and shook his head. "No. The hens will lay without a rooster, but you won't get chicks if there is no rooster."

"I see."

"Wait a second. We won't get chicks if we don't have a rooster?" Gifford asked, looking concerned. "But how will we get more chicks?"

"I guess if your mom wants a rooster, we'll have to get one."

"So this is what you picked up at the post office?"

"Sure is," he said, taking the box and walking the short distance to the picnic table that sat in the yard.

They had supper on it multiple times, especially that spring when the weather was nice.

But for now, he set the box on the table.

"So they mail chicks?" she asked, still trying to wrap her head around the idea that the post office would mail live animals.

"They do. Just before the chick hatches, it sucks up the yolk somehow so that when it hatches out of the egg, it can go for three days without eating or drinking anything. I would imagine that's so that the mama hen who is sitting on the eggs can continue to sit after the first chicks are born and doesn't have to take them directly to get water."

"Interesting. I didn't know that. So they have three days to ship them wherever they're going?"

"That's right," he said as the kids begged to open the box. "These are your mother's chickens, so I think she gets to be the one to do the honors." He handed her his knife.

There was some kind of plastic strap around the box, which kept the lid closed tightly, although Charity could see little beaks poking out of the holes and could hear them chirping loudly.

"Just be careful when you do it, because they might be able to jump out, and while I think we can probably catch them, it won't be good for them. They need the heat of each other to stay warm."

"Oh my goodness. How are we going to take care of them? I don't have—"

"I have all the things you need."

"You do?" Of course he did. He wouldn't have gotten chicks without getting everything that was needed to take care of them.

"It's all out in the addition I put on the barn. That's your chicken coop."

"Are you serious.? You've been spending all this time putting an addition on the barn, and the whole time you've been doing it, you've been intending to use it as a chicken coop for me?"

"You said you wanted chickens."

"I did. But I didn't realize..."

"You should have." They looked at each other, and while the kids were still talking around them, encouraging her to open the box as quickly as she could, it felt like the world faded away and it was just the two of them. She was bemused and charmed and surprised, and he could read all those expressions on her face and looked pleased as punch that he had made her so happy.

It wasn't that he had bought her anything, it was that he had listened, and he had cared, and he had paid attention to her when she was talking and had taken it to heart.

That meant more to her than anything, and she felt like he truly cared about her.

"Thank you," she said, and she didn't just mean thank you for the chicks, she meant thank you for everything.

"Thank you," he said, and she had no idea what he was thanking her for, but he seemed sincere, and then he pointed to the knife. "You better open that, before the kids go crazy."

"Where are we going to put them?"

"I have a place ready over in the addition in the barn. We can head over there, but you want to peek inside first?"

"I'd love to. I can't wait to see what they look like. You said Rhode Island Red? I assume those are red chickens?"

"They are, but the chicks are going to be orange and yellow. They won't be red until they shed their baby feathers, around four to six weeks."

"You sound like you've done this a time or two."

"Back when I first bought the farm, I had several batches of chicks, but I was always drowning in eggs and giving them away, which wasn't terrible, but it was a lot of hassle to try to take care of everything, and I just couldn't keep up."

"Well, now that you have a wife and five kids, you shouldn't lack for people to help you out."

"That's what I figured." He grinned at her.

She snapped off the plastic tie and handed the knife back to him. Then, she carefully lifted the corner of the lid.

The chicks were adorable, peeping and blinking as the light slowly filtered into their tight home.

"Oh. They're adorable." She didn't touch them, although she was tempted, because she didn't want all the kids to think they needed to touch them too.

"I have water and feed over in the barn. When we get them out of the box, we'll dip their beaks in the water, to show them where it is. I've never had a problem with chicks finding the water, but I've always just dipped their beaks in one at a time to give them a taste of it, so they don't die of thirst before they get it figured out."

"They're probably two or three days old and right at the limit of what they can survive."

"Exactly. And shipping is a little bit stressful on them, although that's why you have to get at least fifteen, so that they stay warm without the heat light."

"You have a heat light too?"

"I do. We'll keep it on them for the first four weeks. After they grow their adult feathers, they'll be able to keep themselves warm without it."

"Wow. Okay. My goodness," she murmured, unable to resist putting one finger out and touching a downy head. So soft, so delicate.

"Let me!" Banks said.

"No, chicks are one animal that are better off if they're not handled a whole lot. So it's best if we just look and don't touch." Wilson said that matter-of-factly, but he probably understood how difficult it was going to be for Banks especially to not touch.

He was at that age where he wanted to touch everything, although thankfully he was past the stage where he wanted to touch it all and put it in his mouth too.

"All right, guys, let's head over to the barn. Gifford, if it's okay with your mom, you can carry the box of chicks over."

"That's fine with me. Should I put the lid back on?"

They were so cute huddled together, and she wanted to be able to look at them, but she remembered what he had said about them jumping out.

"Yeah. You better cover them up, and then Gifford needs to be careful not to jostle them too much."

"I've got it." He sounded so grown-up and competent.

Charity glanced at him, looking so serious as he picked the box up, careful to do exactly what Wilson had said. She wasn't quite sure why he was having so much trouble in school. It didn't seem to be any one thing, he just wasn't getting good grades, didn't always pay attention in class, and sometimes the teacher had to send a note home from school that he had pushed someone down at recess or had been mouthy to the teacher.

Charity assumed that all had something to do with his dad leaving and all the other changes in his life, but she wasn't sure. And she definitely didn't know what to do about it.

Regardless, he seemed very enamored with the new chicks and proud of his role carrying them over. Charity would have to remember to thank Wilson for the extra attention that he had been giving Gifford. Gifford seemed to thrive under the little bit of responsibility that he was allowed to have. Maybe that would pull him back from whatever bad path he was traveling down.

They made it to the barn, and sure enough, Wilson had indeed made an entire chicken coop, with boxes for laying and bars for roosting, and in the middle, he had a little area sectioned off with a heat light over top and feed and water close by.

The heat light was on, and everything was ready for the chicks to come out.

"All right, we're going to let your mom do this, and if she thinks Gifford and Banks are old enough to help, they can do it as well. The rest of us are just going to watch. Maybe someday it will be our turn."

"But I want to help!" Lavinia said.

"And I'm sure you can, when you get a little bit bigger," Charity said, not wanting Wilson to have to be the bad guy all the time.

The little girls fussed a bit, but Gifford and Banks were so excited about pulling them out, and dipping their beaks in the water, and then allowing them to run around. Soon all fifteen were out, and they realized they had an extra one.

"Maybe they sent an extra one in case one died. Every once in a while, we do lose one."

"Oh boy. We have sixteen." She hated to show her ignorance, but she had to ask. "How many eggs will we get from them every day?"

"If we were a commercial layer facility, where we could tightly control the amount of daylight they had, and the feed and other environmental factors, we could have them up to ninety-five percent, which means that ninety-five percent of them would lay one egg a day. But for what we're going to do, it'll be good if we get eighty percent, which means eighty percent of sixteen, so that many eggs each day once they start laying."

"Well. My goodness. I guess you guys better start eating a lot of eggs."

"They're nice to give away. You can't sell them, because they're not USDA inspected, but you can give them away, or you can take donations for them."

"Wow. Maybe I can use them in my baking?"

"I don't think you can do that either, but we'll have to check the regulations and see."

"All right. Whether I can or not, it's going to be fun," she said, feeling excited and happy and so totally seen, like Wilson knew exactly what to do in order to make her smile.

She wasn't sure what she could do to make it up to him, but it was definitely something she was praying about.

Chapter Twenty-Four

May 26

School had gotten out a week prior, and it seemed like adding Gifford into the mix had made everything more chaotic.

Or maybe it was just Wilson trying to figure out an excuse as to why he had forgotten their anniversary the day before.

He had determined that he was going to spend at least one day pampering his wife or doing his best to pamper her, and he had made it through the first four months, but he had totally dropped the ball yesterday.

As he and Gifford walked in for lunch, after spending the morning outside checking the cows, tagging a couple of newborn calves, and getting the baler ready to use, he wasn't sure what to do. It seemed like it was too late to fix anything, and really, maybe Charity didn't care. She hadn't said anything, and maybe she forgot herself.

"It smells amazing in here," he said as he opened the door and he and Gifford walked in.

"Daddy!" Lavinia said as she threw herself at his legs.

The sound never ceased to make him smile. She'd started calling him that maybe a month or two prior. First her, and then Serafina and Evans had followed suit. Banks had said it maybe once or twice, and Wilson had watched as Gifford had carefully studied his younger siblings as they accepted him and called him Dad.

He wasn't sure that Charity didn't have something to do with it, but if she did, she wasn't admitting it.

But to be fair, he hadn't asked. He kind of wanted to think that the kids had done it on their own, but the idea that Charity had encouraged them was also encouraging to him.

In all the time that they'd been married, as far as he knew, she hadn't heard a word out of her ex-husband.

"Did you help make lunch?" he asked Lavinia as he picked her up and hugged her, then settled her on his hip.

She was going to be starting kindergarten with Banks the next year. It was odd to have both of them in the same class, but from the way their birthdays fell, it was the accurate way, although he and Charity had talked about holding Lavinia back a year so Banks would have a year to himself.

They had eventually decided that it wouldn't be fair to Lavinia to keep her back, and it might be good for Banks to have his sister with him.

Maybe they were making the wrong decision, but that's what parenting was, doing the best a person could, even while knowing that you were sure to make mistakes.

He hoped it was the best decision. He didn't want to screw these kids up any more than what they'd already been messed up when their dad abandoned them.

It had definitely been hard on Gifford, but Wilson prayed for him nightly and felt like maybe he would eventually come around.

"Mom made your favorite. It's a recipe that Grandma gave her a long time ago."

Wilson looked over Lavinia's head and exchanged a smile with Charity. A long time ago was a couple of months. But he supposed to a five-year-old that really was a long time.

"I forgot our anniversary yesterday. Happy anniversary a day late." He figured he might as well admit it right away, rather than beating around the bush.

"Oh my goodness. I totally forgot too." She looked around. "You wouldn't think one more kid would make that much of a difference."

"I think she's blaming it on you, Gifford," Wilson said, ruffling the boy's hair and grinning at him.

"I've got broad shoulders," Gifford said, sounding so much like himself that Wilson had to pause for a moment.

It was amazing what the kids picked up and how much of himself he saw in them, even though they weren't biologically his. He loved that though, even while it made him feel like he wasn't worthy to be sharing a home with them. What if he led them wrong?

He supposed there wasn't any better way to keep a man on the straight and narrow than to have five small children staring at him constantly, watching his every move.

"I know you do, son," he said, using the word son as an endearment.

Gifford didn't bristle as he had been afraid that he might. Instead, he just grinned bigger.

"If it's okay with you, I'm gonna call my mom and see if she can come over, and I'm gonna take my wife out for supper tonight."

"I don't know. Can we go out on a date if it's not our anniversary?" she asked, smiling so he knew that she was teasing him.

"Let's try it and see," he said, and she laughed.

"That pretty much is our idea of wild, isn't it?"

"That, and getting chicks," he said, knowing how much joy she found in them. There were several times where he found her just sitting in the chicken coop watching the baby chicks run around and enjoying them. He asked her what she was doing, and she really couldn't say, other than she just loved sitting and watching them.

He'd actually spent some time sitting beside her, not saying anything, just enjoying what she enjoyed. He could kinda see what she saw in it, although he supposed he was less interested in the chicks and more interested in seeing a tractor drive across the field. Driving it himself across the field was really what got him.

He loved that feeling of...he wasn't even sure how to describe it, and he figured that that might be something along the lines of what Charity felt with the chicks. Regardless, he had spent some time doing what she loved, just because he thought that he would really like to have her spend some time doing what he loved, although he understood that she couldn't exactly leave the kids and come running out to spend time in the field with him.

He asked his mom before he washed his hands, and she texted back almost immediately that she had already committed to watching Gilbert's kids, although she could do it later in the week.

After he prayed, and they'd gotten the kids all served, he said, "Mom can't make it tonight. She'll do it later in the week, or... How would you feel about having hot dogs around the fire tonight?"

The kids all cheered, and Charity smiled.

"I think that's perfect," she said, and he could tell from her happy smile she was serious. She loved doing things with the whole family just as much as he did, and they tried to include their children in whatever they did. Every time she fed the chicks, she took Lavinia and Serafina with her. Sometimes even Evans went along. He tagged along behind; it was pretty amazing how much he had grown since Christmas.

They'd really grown on Wilson. All the kids had. Although, that was almost overshadowed by the way he felt about Charity. Unfortunately, he had to be careful, because they weren't even halfway through the year that the pastor had said he needed to wait. He couldn't risk ruining everything he was building by moving too soon.

It was probably for the best that they were going to be doing a campfire as a family. Having Charity all to himself was way too dangerous.

Chapter Twenty-Five

June 25

"Do you mind if my mom comes over with Gilbert's kids tonight?"

Charity looked up from where she was working at the counter, cleaning up from lunch.

The kids had gone to play. That was one really nice thing about the farm versus living in town. The kids could go outside, and they knew they had to stay in sight of the house at all times. She could look out from any window and keep an eye on them. The only one who wasn't allowed out with everyone else was Evans, and she had already taken him up for his afternoon nap.

"Of course. That would be wonderful." She loved it when all the cousins got together, and her children loved having extra people over.

"I know that's a lot of extra work for you, and I also know that we're supposed to go out tonight, but Mom got the kids unexpectedly."

"I don't mind at all. I know sometimes she has gotten our kids unexpectedly, and she's always been fine with it. We'll just stay home and enjoy having family time with them. Because eight kids is way more than anyone should have to deal with alone."

"I know my mom can handle it, but I hate asking her."

"You don't have to. I know things aren't going very well for Gilbert." She had heard that from the sisters-in-law when they got together for Sunday dinner after church. Gilbert was often absent, and who could blame him, after he lost his wife so tragically around Christmastime. But his children were suffering, and Charity felt terrible for them. Of course, Gilbert couldn't really help his kids if he needed help himself.

"I appreciate you being willing to roll with it. This is two months in a row, though, that we've missed our anniversary."

"There will be other months that we can celebrate. Family is more important."

"I guess I don't disagree, but I feel like it's not really fair to you."

"Just plan something for sure for next month."

"All right. July, here we come," he said, and she grinned and nodded.

Chapter Twenty-Six

July 25

"We're still on for tonight?" Wilson asked as they finished up breakfast. He enjoyed having the kids home and was dreading the fact that they were going back to school in less than a month. Although he would enjoy having more time alone with his wife, the idea of losing three of the kids was... depressing.

"We sure are. We planned it last month, remember?"

"I do," he said, putting the dishes in the sink and grabbing the rag to wipe the table.

Her phone buzzed, and she pulled it out, setting the milk down on the counter while she read the message.

"Wilson?" she said tentatively as she looked up, and he could tell from the tone of her voice that something happened.

"What is it?" he said immediately, straightening, the rag in his hand. He could watch the kids if she needed to go help somebody. Or... Maybe someone needed him. He could take one or two of the kids with him. Gifford was always good to go. And Banks and Lavinia ought to be able to go with him as well. He figured pretty soon Serafina and even little Evans would all want to go any time he left the farm. Even if he was just feeding cattle or doing mundane chores, the kids loved to follow him around. And he enjoyed the teaching time with them.

"The grocery store in town just said that someone came and asked if they could order ten dozen of my gobs. They want them for this evening."

She looked down at her phone and read it aloud. "'I know that that is really short notice, but I have a customer standing here in front of me, and I wanted to know whether it would be possible for you to do it or not? She'd like to pick them up by nine o'clock this evening.'"

"Wow. That's a lot of gobs."

"I know. And… I could do it, but you and I have a date."

"Well, maybe we can spend our date making gobs?"

"You don't want to do that," she said, tilting her head and giving him an exasperated look.

"As long as I'm with you, I'll do anything, which is better than anything I could do without you." He meant that with his whole heart. She seemed to understand that he was serious, because she shrugged.

"I might be upset if you want to cancel our date just so that you can go do some kind of emergency work…"

"No, you wouldn't. Last month, we canceled our date because my brother wasn't watching his children and got my mother to do it, and my mother wanted to come here, so you and I stayed home, remember? That was me."

"I remember."

"You didn't complain at all. Not even a little bit. In fact, you acted like you had the time of your life." He had really appreciated that. She hadn't complained or acted put out at all. Even though she had to have been looking forward to going out. He knew how much she enjoyed it.

"We could take a rain check," she said, lifting her arms up.

"Somehow, that never happens."

"True."

"The three older children will be in school, and even if Mom has Gilbert's kids, they will be in school too. So we could plan a lunch date, for sure."

"All right. Let's do that."

"And next month, you and I will make it up together."

"All right. It's a deal."

Wilson watched as she turned back to the sink. He knew she was excited about her business doing so well, and he had to say he was happy for her. And while he knew that they wouldn't have any privacy tonight, it was probably a good thing. Although... At night, he'd been dreaming more and more of kissing his wife. It seemed like his every waking thought was consumed with that, and at night, he couldn't get away from it either.

He took a deep breath and turned back to the table, wiping it absentmindedly, while he thought about how much time he had left until next Christmas.

Chapter Twenty-Seven

August 25

"I'll see you guys this evening. No hurry to get home, because the kids are getting off the bus here, and Amy and Jones will be around to give me a hand if I need it." Marjorie smiled at them as they walked off the porch, Evans holding tight to one hand and Serafina holding tight to the other. Evans had turned two. He was becoming such a little boy and didn't look like a baby at all anymore.

Charity sighed. She didn't really miss the baby stage exactly, but in a way, she kind of did. Because he was getting more independent and needed her less and less. Of course, it was going to be years before he didn't need her at all, but he definitely was becoming his own little independent man.

"They're going to be fine," Wilson said with a grin. "Has it been so long since we've been alone together that you're nervous?"

"It has been several months, not including those few times that we've managed to sneak together while the kids were sleeping."

They grinned together, knowing that they had gone out to the barn and worked on a tractor a couple of times, and he helped her bake after the kids had gone to sleep at night. Several times during naptime, they'd go do some chores on the farm together as well, but this was the first time in a really long time that they were going out, just the two of them, and they had the whole day.

"So you said you had something planned?" he said as they got in the pickup.

"Yes, but since you're driving, I can't keep it a surprise until we get there. Unless you're going to let me?"

"You can if you want to," he said, smiling, as he started the pickup. But he didn't put it into drive, as though waiting on her decree.

"I know you've wanted to go to the Winchester sale forever, and I found a restaurant that's not very far from there. The sale starts at eleven, so we should have enough time to go eat and then mosey around, look at the animals, and see the whole thing."

"Really? You want to spend the one day that we have together at the sale barn?" he asked, like he couldn't believe it.

"Is that something you want to do?" she asked, although she knew he did. He'd mentioned several times about how much he missed going.

"I actually really would love to go, and I think you'll enjoy it too. And I know that going with you will make it better than it's ever been for me."

"All right then. It's settled." She smiled, satisfied. After all, he'd done so much for her, and every date had been about her. She didn't want this one to be about anything but him. She'd even picked the steakhouse because she knew he liked those types of places. All in all, she thought it was going to be an awesome day.

And she ended up being right. They had a good meal at the steakhouse when it opened at eleven and then enjoyed the auction, although Wilson lamented to her that he should have brought his stock trailer, because there were several heifers that he would like to have bid on.

She encouraged him to go ahead and do it, saying that they had plenty of time to go back and get the trailer and bring it back to pick them up that evening, but he declined.

They stayed until the auction was completely over and walked out of the building hand in hand.

"You know, I really appreciate you doing that. I... I guess there's just something about the auction barn that I really love."

"Even though you didn't buy anything?" she asked, tilting her head and looking up at him, unable to contain the fact that she was very pleased with herself. She felt like maybe she'd finally done something that he enjoyed.

"Yeah, I don't have to buy anything. It's just the atmosphere. Getting together with other farmers, seeing what's for sale, and thinking about all the things that I could do. I don't know, I guess it inspires me."

"Maybe the way looking at recipes online inspires me." She smiled.

"Exactly." He paused for a moment, checked the time, and then said, "We have some time, would you like to take a walk in the park that's across the street?"

"I'd love to," she said, and they headed in that direction. She hadn't even realized there was a park there. It was pretty, with benches and a bubbling brook, and it felt peaceful and quiet and serene.

"The kids would love that," she said, pointing to the jungle gym.

"I was just thinking they would love wading in the creek."

"Yeah, it's kind of sad that they went to school. I miss them."

"I do too. I'm used to having them dogging my steps all day long, and now I turn around, and there's no one there."

"The little ones are with you some."

"Yeah. And I really enjoy it. I like having them, but I do miss turning around and getting Gifford to grab me something or, I don't know, he's just a great help."

"I'm happy to hear it. I hope he has a better year this year than he did last."

"I hope so too," he said as they stopped on a bridge, leaning against the railing. "But I think we fall into the trap of every other married couple. Talking about kids when we actually get some time alone."

"We kind of do need to talk about them, but you're right. We should talk about something else."

They stared at each other, and there was a little voice in Charity's head that whispered that she should tell him that they'd been married long enough that he could kiss her. But then, her old fears took over and she thought maybe he didn't want to, maybe he didn't want a relationship like that, or maybe he wasn't interested in her that way, and she kept her mouth closed.

Then, to her surprise, he lifted a hand up and brushed her hair back, the way he had back when they were first married. She couldn't remember why he had done it then, but she closed her eyes now, just enjoying the feel of his hand on her skin and hair before it disappeared.

She opened her eyes and turned immediately and leaned on the railing.

She should say something, but she couldn't think of what to say.

It was easier to talk when she was looking out over the water, so she didn't turn her head but said the words that she'd been wondering for a while.

"Do you think you'll ever be attracted to me?"

She held her breath. She told herself that she could take it if he said no, that she would rather have the truth than spend the rest of her life wondering.

There was silence, complete and total silence other than the babbling of the brook and an occasional chirping of a bird. The breeze lifted her hair, calm and serene. She thought about the good date they'd had and wondered why she had chosen to ruin it just now.

"I'm not sure what to say. I guess...what makes you think I'm not attracted to you?"

Wow. How could he think she thought that he was? Where did she begin? It was awkward to talk about, but she'd started it, and she wanted answers. She couldn't be afraid to continue the conversation.

"You never touch me. You...don't kiss me, we don't sleep together. I thought it was going to be a real marriage, but...I'm not complaining. Please don't think I am." She turned to look at him then, pleading on her face, because she really did love the relationship that they had, she just...wanted to be a wife too.

He stood staring at her, shock on his face, and then he shook his head, running a hand over his hair like he was agitated. He took one step forward, then turned around, away from her, like he was gathering his thoughts.

"It's okay. I'm not angry. I'm not mad, and I'm not accusing you of anything, I just...was hoping that maybe sometime in the future?" She left the question open so that he could step in, hoping to make it easier for him to talk. Maybe he could let her down gently, because she knew he wouldn't want to hurt her. He really did think a lot of her. She didn't doubt that.

"So... You judge my attraction by how much I touch you? Whether or not I kiss you? Is that right?"

"Isn't that how you show attraction?" she asked, her brows drawn down as she tried to meet his eyes, but he had one hand hooked around his neck and stared off in the sky.

"I guess it is."

"I'm not accusing you of anything. I'm just saying."

"When's the last time you touched me? Kissed me? Am I to assume that you're not attracted to me either?"

She stopped with her mouth open. And then, after opening and closing it a couple of times and feeling a bit like a fish, she finally said, "I wanted you to take the lead. I told myself that I wasn't going to be forward and push you into anything you didn't want. You already were in a marriage that you didn't want."

"I wanted it!" He turned around and said the words. They were loud, and perhaps several people who were sitting nearby turned their heads, but she barely paid attention.

"It wasn't up to you. I know you did what God wanted."

"No. I know that I said God wanted me to come, and He did, but I told you, I figured out that God wanted it because I needed it, not because you needed me."

"Whatever, so you needed me. But you didn't want me."

"But I do now!"

"I do too." She didn't think they were arguing about whether or not they wanted to be married. "And I'm not confused about whether or not you're going to stay with me. I know you will. You said you would, and I know you keep your word. That's not what I was saying."

"I know that wasn't what you're saying, but you were trying to say that I'm not attracted to you, and it's not true."

His words hung there, as both of them were quiet. Neither one of them saying anything as they stared at each other, the truth hanging in the air between them.

She tilted her head, wondering how to reconcile what he said. She knew he wouldn't lie about what he actually did want. But they didn't match up.

"When we got married, that day as I was walking the pastor to the door, he told me that since we didn't court before we were married, I should give you time to get used to me, not come on too strong. I think he knows how men are. And that's me. It's true. I definitely want the physical side of marriage, but I know that women aren't the same as men. And I asked him how long I should wait, and he told me a year."

"A year?" she cried out, unable to hold her words any longer, although she wanted to argue with him that women and men might be different, but that didn't mean that she didn't want the same thing that he did.

"It didn't seem unreasonable to me. He said that was how long a lot of couples typically waited as they court and get to know each other, in fact that's probably on the short end of modern day."

"But we haven't really done anything the way modern-day people do it."

"I know. But I didn't want to push you. I didn't want you to be forced to do something you didn't want to do."

"I see."

"I still don't."

"I haven't had to do anything I didn't want to do," she said.

"That's exactly how I wanted it."

They stood staring at each other.

"But there were a lot of things I wanted to do but that didn't happen."

"Such as?" he asked immediately, his eyes narrowed, as though he were thinking back, trying to figure out how he had missed something.

"Like kissing. I really like kissing. I like cuddling. I like...the idea of doing it with you."

His hand came up again, only this time, his knuckles brushed her cheek before his fingers wrapped around her neck, and he stepped closer.

"Are you serious? Are you just saying that because today has been all about me, and you think this is something I want too?"

"No. I'm saying it because I didn't think you were attracted to me because you never touch me. We don't kiss. There's nothing."

"And now you know why. Pastor Connelly said to wait. I didn't want to do things on my own, he said that together you and I should build a strong foundation. That we wouldn't regret waiting and building something that was built on more than physical."

"Maybe you and I could decide that together?"

"I think so."

"Okay. How do you feel about kissing?"

"I've wanted to for a long time. At first, it was all I could think about during the day, every time I saw you, and then I started dreaming about it at night. Now, that's pretty much all I dream about."

"Well," she said, putting a hand on either side of his waist, and then taking a step closer, and moving one hand up so that she buried her fingers in his hair. "What do you say we start right now?"

Her breath was a little shaky, because she was afraid that he was still going to tell her no. Maybe what the pastor had suggested would overrule what she did, but she thought they had a pretty solid foundation, and she didn't see any reason why they couldn't kiss. Plus, she wanted to. And if he did too, that settled it in her mind.

"I suppose, if that's what you want. After all, I've wanted it for a long time." His lips came down, and they brushed against her temple. She closed her eyes, but she remembered the forehead kiss that he'd given her before. It was sweet, and she liked it, but that wasn't the kind of kissing she was talking about.

She rolled her head just a bit so that his lips moved down to her cheek.

She opened her eyes, and she said, "You're almost there."

She felt him smile against her cheek, and her lips turned up too.

"I'm trying to kiss someone. You have to stop making me laugh."

"I think laughter is a part of it."

"I think it's an important part."

They didn't talk any more after that, as his lips came down on hers, and she didn't even think that there might be people watching or that maybe they should have chosen a different time. She just thought how bright and good it felt to finally be kissing her husband, Wilson, the man she loved. With all her heart and soul and everything she had.

She lost track of time and couldn't have said how long it was until he finally lifted his head and ran his lips across her cheek. "I love you. I've wanted you for a really long time, and can I just say I love kissing you?"

"Yeah. You can say that. And you can say the whole part about loving me again, I'm not going to argue about it."

"I love you."

"I love you too. I love kissing you and hope that we might get to do it a good bit more."

"Maybe, if it's okay with you, I'll move upstairs today."

"If I'd have known you were going to do that, I would have taken you to the sale barn in January."

He let out a laugh. "Wife, those are the most romantic words anyone has ever said to me."

"I try." She smiled, and then his lips covered hers again, and they didn't talk for a really long while.

Join Jessie's list and be the first to know about new releases and sales on her books!

Read Christmas Dreams, the fourth book from Mistletoe Meadows, featuring Gilbert and Summer. Gilbert never intended to offer to allow Summer to live on the farm with his children and him. But they love her and he soon finds himself drawn to her as well. Will the holiday spirit help give these two a chance at love?

Sneak Peek of Christmas Dreams

Gilbert McBride pushed away from his desk and leaned back in his chair, putting his hands behind his head and looking up at the ceiling.

He'd done it. Finally. After more than a year of relentless work and effort, blood, sweat, and tears, he had brought his equipment rental business back from the brink of bankruptcy and turned it into a profitable business machine once more.

His wife's cancer and subsequent death had almost ruined it. Not just because all of Gilbert's energy was fixated on being with his wife and children during that difficult time, but because his office manager had been embezzling money. She offered discounts to people who paid in cash, then pocketed the cash, not mentioning it in the books, of course, and hadn't paid any of the monthly bills.

By the time his lifelong friend had been propositioned by her, the company was on the verge of going belly up. That was just about the time that Gilbert's wife had died.

That was Christmas, one year ago.

In the last year, he worked relentlessly, building things up again, because he felt he owed it to his three children to provide as stable of a home as he could. Granted, in the last year, he hadn't been around much, but they had been well taken care of by his mother, who had raised six children of her own and could certainly handle three more.

It was true he felt guilty, but he also felt like he had no choice. If he was going to be a good father and provide for them, he had to do something to save his business, and it was going to have to be radical, and he was going to have to be all in.

But he knew if he put a whole lot of effort into it and gave himself a year, he could get the ship righted, and then once that happened, he would have time to spend with his children again.

The profit from last month would enable him to have a sizable down payment to put on a house, they could move out of his mother's place, and he and his children would become a family again.

He hadn't wanted to do it that way, but he hadn't seen any other way to save the business and his family. Losing the business would have meant being in debt for the rest of his children's childhoods, and he hadn't wanted that stress on his family. Losing their wife and mother had been enough.

He knew that there were people who criticized him for not being there for his children after their mother's death. He had taken two full weeks to spend entirely with them before he plunged himself into the business, but...he couldn't do both. And while his children were more important than any business, he also was commanded to be the provider for his family. He couldn't just let that go, as much as he might have wanted to hold each one of his children close for as long as he could.

His phone buzzed and he sat up, grabbing it from off the desk where he'd set it, and saw that it was his realtor calling. He'd put in a request last week for a farm, preferably one that could raise horses, since the therapy riding that they'd done seemed to make his children happy, and he wanted it in the general area where his mother and siblings lived in Mistletoe Meadows. Ideally, he had told his realtor, he wanted to be moved in by Christmas. Considering that it was currently October, he thought he might have been a little bit demanding, but in his experience, it was best to say what he actually wanted, rather than settling. Who knew, maybe the Lord would open the door and see fit to bless him and his children with the perfect location.

"Hello?" he said, standing up out of his chair and walking around until he stood in front of the window, looking out on the buildings of Harrisonburg, Virginia. It was a nice town but bigger than what he was used to, and there was no need for him to stay, now that the business was in hand.

He could go back to Mistletoe Meadows where he really wanted to be.

"Gilbert. I'm so glad I caught you. You know what a tight market we're in right now, and I told you when you gave me your dream list that more than likely we'd not be able to find anything, but...I am very pleased to inform you that I have advance knowledge of a farm, just like you asked for, coming onto the market. It should be listed later today or tomorrow at the latest. And it's currently being used as a horse therapy facility, so horses are definitely a centerpiece."

"Just like I requested," he said, feeling very satisfied. He put a hand on the wall and leaned against it, looking off at the brilliant blue October sky. "You can send me the information, but I trust that you found what I wanted. I'll go see the property as soon as you can arrange it, and I'll come prepared to make an offer on the spot."

He had everything lined up and did not intend to dillydally around. He wanted to get his family back together. He didn't want to bring his children back to Harrisonburg, putting them back in school there, when he knew he was going to be moving them and wouldn't have time to be mom and dad while he rescued his business, so they had spent a lot of time at his mother's house. It was also good for the kids to be out in the country where they could run around versus the town home that his late wife had preferred.

That had already sold, which is what had given him the money to help bring his business back in the black and eventually what had enabled him to get the down payment for the farm he intended to purchase.

Still, the downside had been that he hadn't been able to have his children with him since he'd been sleeping in the apartment above the shop, except on weekends and occasionally during the week when he was able to make the drive to Mistletoe Meadows.

"I've already done it. I have us scheduled for a showing tomorrow morning at nine AM. If that doesn't suit, I can reschedule. Just let me know."

"That's perfect."

He made a mental note to talk to his new office manager. The man had come highly recommended, and Gilbert intended to oversee everything. He had no wife to get cancer or, before that, to cheat on him.

His lips pressed together. No one knew about that. He hadn't told a soul about the letter that he found that had changed everything between his wife and him.

"All right. I'll see you bright and early tomorrow morning," she said before they said goodbye and hung up.

He texted his office manager immediately, letting him know that he would be in late in the morning if at all.

Sending the text off, he leaned against the wall and contemplated all the things that he needed to do. He felt like the business was a priority, but now that it was taken care of, his children were going to take center stage. Lucas was almost thirteen, which was a delicate age, and he needed his father.

Gilbert had spent as much time with him as he could over the summer, but he appreciated his brother-in-law helping out as well. Especially when he couldn't be there.

Then there was Marissa, who followed her grandmother around everywhere and thought the woman walked on water. Gilbert wasn't entirely sure that his mother didn't walk on water. She seemed to be almost perfect. Young for her age, and resourceful, although she was definitely moving slower and getting older. He didn't like to think about it, because his mother had been the one constant in his life. The person he could always depend on to do right and to be there for him. When his wife was in the hospital, his mother dropped everything to do whatever he needed her to—watch the kids, make food, give him a ride if he needed it, whatever it was, whatever he asked, she never said no. He owed her so much more than he could ever repay.

And then there was Robert, who was ten and somewhat quiet. Gilbert didn't know him as well, but he had every intention of changing that, and soon.

Sign up for Jessie's newsletter! Get a free book, access to exclusive bonus content, get fun and funny updates on her life on the farm and more!

A Gift from Jessie

View this code through your smart phone camera to be taken to a page where you can download a FREE ebook when you sign up to get updates from Jessie Gussman! Find out why people say, "Jessie's is the only newsletter I open and read" and "You make my day brighter. Love, love, love reading your newsletters. I don't know where you find time to write books. You are so busy living life. A true blessing." and "I know from now on that I can't be drinking my morning coffee while reading your newsletter – I laughed so hard I sprayed it out all over the table!"

Claim your free book from Jessie!